Praise for Carter's Debut Novel
I, Sarah Steinway

"... by turns very funny and very serious, confident and uncompromisingly weird. Mary E. Carter has a voice with unquestionable power, and we look forward to reading more from her."
Jewish Book Council

—

"Carter's page-turning portrait of a woman surviving the apocalypse is hauntingly memorable."
Publishers Weekly

—

"In I, Sarah Steinway, our heroine knows just how to use the imaginative technique of midrash to make her points from a Jewish perspective."
Rabbi Jack Shlachter, Judaism for Your Nuclear Family

—

"... Sarah is a compelling character – chatty, spirited, slightly discombobulated ... readers will root for her to keep her head above water."
—*Kirkus Reviews*

—

"The whole book could be considered a postdiluvian midrash." *Rabbi Deborah J. Brin, Mishkan of the Heart*

Other Books by Mary E. Carter

A Non-Swimmer Considers Her Mikvah

I, Sarah Steinway

All Good Tova Goodman Revised Edition

The Three-Day Departure of Mrs. Annette Zinn

A Death Delayed

Agent Orange: Hidden Killer in Vietnam

Electronic Highway Robbery

DIASPORA *of the* DISCOMBOBULATED

DIASPORA *of the* DISCOMBOBULATED

— A Novel—

— Mary E. Carter —

TOVAH
MIRIAM

—

Mary E. Carter
ISBN 979-8-218-23312-9

First Printing
Printed in USA

Cover Art: Photo, Mary E. Carter
Author Photo: Selfie, Mary E. Carter
Book Design: Gary W. Priester
Paintings on pages 230, 234: Mary E. Carter
Photograph on page 127: 1944 World War II Royal Air Force
Service Dress Uniform with U.S. Airforce wings
Photographs on page 55: ShutterStock
Excerpts from Letters, 1944 – 1946 Mary Zimmerman Carter

www.tovah-miriam.com - www.mary-carter.com

“Le cœur a ses raisons que la raison ne connaît point.”

“The heart has its reasons,
for which reason knows nothing of.”

Blaise Pascal

For JH

Chava

1

Before I started writing this book, I asked a variety of my friends if they believed in Guardian Angels. Or not.

I questioned all kinds of people, the observant and the secular: Jewish, Christian, Muslim, and None-of-the-Above. Some of my friends and acquaintances were determined, and even showed off a bit to me, that they were not at all religious. There were a couple of Buddhist aspirants, a couple of Existential throwbacks to Sartre, and several yoga enthusiasts who could quote Patanjali and B.K.S Iyengar.

"Do you believe in Guardian Angels?"

The responses I got to my question were a surprise. Half did. Half did not — believe in Guardian Angels. But what was surprising to me was the intensity with which they expressed either their belief or disbelief in Guardian Angels. Whether yes or no, their opinions were supported by very strong rationales. Yet, *rationales*, is not quite the right word. Strong opinions, yes, from both camps. Surprisingly strong emotions, from both the believers and the non-believers.

But here is what I found most interesting: the non-believers had long and somewhat peevish arguments for their beliefs in non-belief. As well, these non-believers did not have many rational bits of evidence or scientific thinking, just plenty of emotion. The believers had similarly strong beliefs that, yes, there are definitely such beings as Guardian Angels. But again, no evidence or logical proof points. Just plain and definite, and vociferous: belief.

I would not say that either side provided me with anything tangible about Guardian Angels. Evidence was missing on both sides.

Also of interest in my friend survey, some of the very convinced believers were a complete surprise for me. People who I would never have thought in a million years would believe in Guardian Angels did believe in them and quite passionately. They answered instantly:

"Yes!"

Talking about Guardian Angels may be talking about an unseen, unproven, immaterial entity that is not really an entity at all. Pixies, gnomes, elves, goblins, sprites, fairies, little folk. Angels, archangels, fallen angels. Flying, falling, floating — are they for real or are they mere imaginary figments?

Oh, for heavens' sake!

Why? Why believe in Guardian Angels? Then too, conversely: Why not?

I couldn't quite bring myself to demand more from my friends. Already the non-believers were annoyed at my silly question. And the believers were looking away, seemingly bored — or was it a kind of guardedness? — backing away from my question as if it were just too personal or incriminating. Funny I should use the word *guardedness*. In any case, I wasn't sure I could muster my mental energy to bother either camp any further on the issue. My friends were losing patience with me.

But I couldn't stop wondering: why yes and why no? What's going on here?

2

Yet, right here, in real life, right now, a Guardian Angel stands before me and seems to need to speak to me. She is standing right in front of me, wings trembling. She is actually here in my studio. How can this be? How can she be standing here in the morning light, standing right here in front of the long wall in my studio where I display my paintings?

This is important. I better take notes of this encounter.

I live in the northern escarpment of the Sandia Range in New Mexico. I sit in my studio with its four large windows facing west and two smaller windows at the top of the east wall. When the sky is clear of brown haze from the Belt of Venus, it is not impossible to see sixty miles to the west from my studio here.

Yet, too, it is not impossible to see and to hear my visitor, a Guardian Angel, right now, right here, in front of me. She is persistent, urgent, wings atremble. I can see she needs to tell me something. I gesture for her to sit on my sofa. I will listen to her without hesitation. She is an embodiment. Just like me. But how can this be? What is going on here? Is she an hallucination? Am I? Maybe we both need a cup of coffee. I wonder: do Guardian Angels like coffee?

3

She graciously accepts my gesture to sit on the sofa. She is magnificent in her disarray, with a curious and somewhat tattered splendor. She establishes eye-contact with me. I see that she wears a name tag. It is one of those familiar plastic ID cards, worn around the neck by the attendees of corporate gatherings — conventions, annual sales meetings, marketing pep rallies. I see that her name is Hannah-Naomi. Below this is her company name: Gig Guardian Angels LLC.

She arranges her long angelic gown around her knees. It floats around her, diaphanous, lifted by invisible angelic breezes I suppose. It is threadbare around her ankles, worn rather than torn, however. A slender bare leg obtrudes from ragged slits. She possesses several of the expected ethereal clichés of angelic fashion as represented in the paintings of the Renaissance or as seen on the familiar walls and ceilings of cathedrals. Unlikely small wings propel her up and down as she adjusts her posture. She is fidgeting a bit. I suppose it's a moment of latent angelic energy as she seems to be settling into a comfortable posture for further conversation.

She wears her hair all this-way-and-that-way, clutched and grabbed with too many claw-clips, clipped backwards and sideways, clumping long locks of her hair into the nape of her neck, to the crown of her head, dozens of them, all of them ineffectual. Her tresses are tenuous and scatter in the breezes from her lips as she speaks and moves her head. She blows floating stray locks of hair distractedly away, like blowing kisses but, rather more to the point, she blows away and upward smoke from a Camel cigarette.

4

Is this really happening? Am I about to have a chat with a real live Guardian Angel? I am sure that she is sitting here in front of me, lounging comfortably on my sofa. Am I nuts??? I must be crazy. I pull up a chair alongside the sofa. My guest seems quite comfortable. Now she starts to speak to me.

Hannah-Naomi

1

Good morning, Chava. Thank you for receiving me here in your own home. My name is Hannah-Naomi. Hannah is a Hebrew name meaning *favor or grace*. And my other name, Naomi, is also Hebrew and means *beautiful, pleasant, delightful*.

I see that your name is Chava, which in its essence means: *Life*. And so, between the two of us here, there exists all there is to this world: the favor of life and an enlightening mood of beauty and delight.

Thus, even our names are significant. Our names hint at an amicable joining of our selves as we share, perhaps a cup of coffee, and discuss, or maybe gently debate, the great wisdoms of our separate selves.

I am a Guardian Angel.

I have been a Guardian Angel since before recorded time. I was a Guardian Angel long centuries before this

Uncommon Era. I have served as Guardian Angel to soldiers, sailors, warriors, mothers, babes and blades of grass. I have provided guardianship for harvesting grain, davening for water, and for nourishing character in untested souls. Now, still here, I am provided with new tools to perform the ancient tasks of guardianship. That is why I am here before you today. We Guardian Angels have been called transcendent, supernal, stellar, and most importantly, we've been called just in the nick of time.

2

Guardian Angels are adept in the formation of life-saving coincidences. We can shift into swift action in the redirection of oncoming traffic, if needs be. Witness this familiar scenario:

There is a screech as a car swings erratically over the double line. An advancing truck veers sideways onto the shoulder to avoid the oncoming vehicle. The car glides, safely, onto its own side of the road. The truck brakes to a gentle stop on the other side. The car and the truck are now safely out of danger. The drivers are both safe. Catastrophe has been averted by mere inches. Both drivers then shout:

"*Wow. I must have a Guardian Angel.*"

You like? A life-saving coincidence? Or was that a nudge from a Guardian Angel? Unbelievers will say it was a mere lucky coincidence. Believers will say: "See? See? There are such things as Guardian Angels.

That was a nudge from my very own Guardian Angel."

3

We are entering an era of the new Gig Economy. With it come possibilities of an entire new way to work in our roles as Guardian Angels. In fact, I am now a freelance entrepreneur. I have at my wingtips new digital tools to enhance the traditional tools of my trade as a Guardian Angel. I call my enterprise Gig Guardian Angels and I have already had some success making use of my own Freewill, multi-tasking, and communicating with my charges online, from the cloud. With email I can communicate directly with my charges. I can use my trusty old trick of an Angelic nudge and I can aid them in solving problems with my well-used gift of foresight into future events. All of this I can do using the tools of this dawning digital era. My charges will be unable to unsubscribe to my email blasts and so they will not forget or misplace valuable information I send to them from the cloud.

Much what I will do in my guardianship duties will depend upon memory. My own memories and the memories of two of my charges, for example. There will be much memory work involved as I advise and guide them over their lifetimes. I refer here to two particular charges of mine: Artemisia Gershom and with Gershom Holder. They are both artists.

To understand how memory affects the relationship

between a Guardian Angel and her charges, you need to know how memory works. You must understand how memory is stored and how it is retrieved. How does memory, once retrieved, affect further actions of a human being? The human memory system inherently influences how the Guardian Angel uses the new Guardian Angelic tools of the digital era.

4

There is, mysteriously, a conundrum in human memory. How and what gets remembered will, to some extent, be revealed by a person when they think about or talk about or act upon their retrieved memories. But memory is essential in the work of a long-term Guardian Angel. Your human being must be able to remember and to retranscribe memories and use them in future actions. In the case of an artist, memories may nourish the artist's creative process. An artist may literally draw upon memories to create, for instance, a painting.

This is particularly important as a person ages. Memories seem to contain more and different images and conclusions, the older a person becomes. And a human being may see old memories in a fresh light, influenced by the accretions of decades of new life experiences. This needs to be gently prodded by the Guardian Angel so that the human mortal finally *gets* — in the sense of fully understanding — an old memory.

Here. I have it in my notes:

Sigmund Freud had a lot to say about this phenomenon:

> *"I am working on the assumption that our psyche is subjected from time to time to a rearrangement in accordance with fresh circumstances — a* ***retranscription*** *— Memory is present not once but several times over . . . the successive* ***retranscriptions*** *represent the psychic achievements of successive epochs of life . . ."*

It is one of the jobs of a Guardian Angel to nudge the human being toward new retranscriptions of old memories.

I struggle now with the need to make abundantly clear the role of memory and memory retrieval in the job of a Guardian Angel to a human soul. In order to gain the attention of both of my artists over their lifetimes, I have frequently turned to the tool of retranscription of memory.

5

I should confess now that I became a Fallen Angel at one point. For a time, I became a human woman, vulnerable to all the wiles of love and of desire. I am embarrassed to reveal this to you, Chava. It was a process of much confusion for me and for my charges, Artemisia and Gershom. But that drama is for later.

Chava

1

I see, Hannah-Naomi, that you already know who I am. And I vaguely understand why you are here today in my studio. Yet, I am uncertain as to what you intend. It is my usual way to ask questions. Questions upon questions. Not least of which is this: are you for real? Are you truly an embodiment or am I going round the bend? Well, despite my hesitations, I will continue to listen and, despite my fears for my own sanity, I shall sit here and pay attention to you.

You have shared with me some of the tools of your trade that you use as a Gig Guardian Angel. But what about this I ask you:

Where have all the guardian angels gone?

What kind of world is this, now in its last gasps of humanity, of kindness? As I see it, there is no kindness, no gentle prod to keep danger at bay. In fact, quite the opposite: now our world is a very dangerous place.

I despair now. It is May 28, 2022. Where have all the Guardian Angels gone? Reconciliation looks impossible. This world, my world, is in dark despair. If I might have been somewhat disposed to say "yes" they do exist, these Guardian Angels, right now I feel the idiot for thinking this, even for a moment. It's delusional. What an idiot I have been to craft a fiction around any sort of optimism that might have indicated that Guardian Angels do exist. They nudge you into safety. Keep you from danger. But not now. I cannot say that I feel that I have a Guardian Angel who will protect and guide me. Look at this date. I cannot feel that I have a Guardian Angel at this time in history.

Scoffers, winners now in this debate, they are all puffed up and spit at me bitterly and say:

"See! See! There are no such things as Guardian Angels."

I can only lamely reply that the absence of proof is not the proof of absence. How sad.

Where have all the angels gone? I ask again.

Hannah-Naomi makes herself comfortable on my sofa. Spreading her wings along the tops of the pillows, she swings both legs legnthwise onto the seat cushions, sighs, and continues:

Hannah-Naomi

1

Well, Chava, I believe that your mother once instructed you with these words:

"*You have a Guardian Angel.*"

"What does she look like, Mama?"

"Well, little darlin', you won't be able to see her. She will always be just out of your eyesight, moving behind you when you turn your head to look in her direction."

"Does she have wings, Mama?"

"Well, we won't know, will we? She will always be just out of your sight."

Okay.

But this is serious.

Great minds, philosophers, commentators, rabbis, some prophets — yes, maybe they too — the holy and the skeptics — some of them quite level-headed, others not so much — have applied their knowledge and curiosity and wisdom to glean meaning and truth to debatable references to Guardian Angels.

Then again, mothers and grandmothers intone, whispering secrets into their infants' brand-new ears:

"You have a Guardian Angel."

Those words, imprinted into belief and taken as truth into the minds of nascent human children, cannot be mocked. Take seriously your child's belief that asserts that:

"I have a Guardian Angel."

It was simple, declarative, a mother's instruction:

"You have a Guardian Angel."

No philosopher, no teacher, no received commentary ever was so blunt, yet so equivocal. Instruction from a mother supersedes all, or any, holy, or unholy, teaching. Rationalization, argument, or rebuttal count for nothing against a mother saying:

"You have a Guardian Angel."

No need to over-think it. It stands alone, embedded, indelible in a child's mind:

"I have a Guardian Angel."

Chava

1

All right. You have given me the fundamentals for belief in yourself as a Gig Guardian Angel. It sounds like belief comes from mothers and grandmothers. They, who have themselves been thus indoctrinated into their own firm beliefs in Guardian Angels. But surely there must be more to it than that.

2

You know, Hannah-Naomi, I was the difficult student in Torah class. Not one word into the text and I would ask:

"Why does it say *in* the beginning?"

Thinking aloud, I would continue:

"Should it not have said *during* the beginning? That word — *during* — would better communicate that the beginning was perhaps a longish process of events and that that period of time included many phases in the construction and creation of a world which would become inhabited by human beings, animals, weather, landmasses, oceans. You get the point. Or maybe the Torah should have said instead: *In the process of beginning, God created. . .*

Ah, I was the joy of several patient rabbis. That was me. And to my classmates, I was just an annoyance. Who cares? Why does she ask this question now? It's time to go home. What's she even talking about?

So what I am asking right now as I speak with you, Hannah-Naomi, I am asking — like I always did in Torah Study classes — I am asking questions and questions and more questions:

Am I nuts? How can I be sitting here with a real Guardian Angel? Is she real? Here she is, in person with me. She seems to be telling me all about her life as a Guardian Angel. She is harping at me about how she is going to change how Guardian Angels function in this new Gig Economy, in a world that is in no way like what it was in centuries past? And I ask myself: Is this for real? Then I ask my guest:

Hannah-Naomi: you say you have been a Guardian Angel for eons. Can you prove that to me?

Hannah-Naomi

1

You may wonder and ask: what did I even know about being a Guardian Angel during previous eras in the history of Guardian Angels? As I said, and I reiterate, I have been a Guardian Angel since before recorded time, well before this new digitized Gig Economy. Before now, I was a model-Guardian Angel in the old regime of Heavenly Hosts. I had served at the behest of my Creation Director in the guardianship of soldiers, sailors, warriors, mothers, babes, and blades of grass. We did it the old way back then: reporting back and forth for instructions from our Creation Director, never performing more than one task at a time, never using our own Freewill. Up and down ladders we went, always seeking permission and instructions from the Creation Director.

But now we can choose to do things differently. Maybe not all Guardian Angels will elect this new direction for guardianship duties. But for myself, and some of my colleagues, we now can work as Gig Guardian Angels.

Presently, I am in service to two artists. As human beings, both of my charges were strangers borne into a strange land. It was evident, even, in the coincidences of their human names: she is Artemisia Gershom and he is Gershom Holder. I thoroughly believe that I was destined to serve as Guardian Angel to these two human beings, who each share the name of Gershom, which in translation from Hebrew means *a stranger there*.

Additionally, there is the coincidence that both of my charges are the offspring of Pilots in the military during one of the moments of the world when it was at war. It was as if I had received a vision. It was as if I had been placed in the right place at the right time — a coincidence of our three fates, if you will. Some might suggest to me: "Well, it was a message from your Creation Director." We could debate this. But why?

If you believe somewhat at this point that I really am a Guardian Angel, does that mean that you believe I am omniscient? That I know all, see all? Well, hell! I'm just as confused as any mortal would be, on any subject that you can imagine. Ease up. You do not need to reiterate your questioning of me as if I were on the witness stand. You do not need further facts or circumstances and all. This is a story. It's my story. Me, Hannah-Naomi's story. And I shall tell it in whatever haphazard fashion I can muster. I am not perfect. I am not omniscient. But I am a Guardian Angel. So travel a while with me and let's see what we discover.

As my story unfolds, suffice it to say, I know what I am talking about when I compare and contrast being a Guardian Angel in the previous eras with being a Guardian Angel now in this new Gig Economy. I am, to be precise, a Gig Guardian Angel at this moment.

Chava

1

By now, I find that I am paying close attention to Hannah-Naomi's presentation. Is this a speech? Indeed, I am not quite certain. Is she really talking to me? Part of me sees and hears her as an immediate presence, my guest no less. Another part of me glances out the window to secure myself on this planet, looking at these mesas out to the west. I literally *ground* myself by looking away from my guest for a moment. Is this really happening? Am I sitting here in my own studio actively listening to a real Guardian Angel?

I must make clear right here at the beginning of listening to Hannah-Naomi: I am no expert on Jewish beliefs, commentary, scripture. Well, a little bit on Torah, yes. And I have studied devotedly all of the above. I mean well during my explorations. I want to study and have, indeed, pledged to study for the rest of my Jewish life throughout the remainder of whatever life I am vouchsafed. But I am not a Jewish scholar, as such. It is more truthful to say: I am quite an auto-didact about things Jewish. That said, I have studied for several decades now, Jewish commentary, including on the subject of Angels and Angelology.

That I am listening right now to Hannah-Naomi, self-proclaimed Gig Guardian Angel, does not mean I am familiar with all things angelic. In fact, you dear reader, might even conclude, instead, that I've gone round the bend. Senile. Hallucinogenic. And I agree this far: yes, I am a tottering member of what I have jokingly dubbed The Diaspora of the Discombobulated. Confused. Misinformed. Babbling. But nuts? Perhaps. It does seem unlikely that anybody, any human being, wouldn't sound somewhat loony when I tell you that, here in my studio, I am conversing with a real Guardian Angel. She sits here right on my sofa. So am I nuts? Maybe it's time to check me into one of those long-term care facilities for older, read senile, adults.

As with all Jewish commentary, I realize, full and well, that it is my duty to argue. My pledge to my own Jewish life is to question. Patience, I implore. Let's just see where we go and listen, and question, then listen some more to this visitor in my studio, Gig Guardian Angel, Hannah-Naomi.

Now she continues, discursive, further relaxing in my presence, nestled onto my sofa, right here, right now, here in my studio.

Hannah-Naomi

1

My first charge, Artemisia Gershom, was presented to me in the old way — as a duty assignment from the Creation Director. And so I have been her Guardian Angel since she drew her first breath in the cosmic and oxygenated atmosphere of this small blue planet.

My second charge I met many years later when Artemisia was in college. And that coincidence locked me into being the Guardian Angel of yet another human being, named Gershom Holder. Funny how those two possessed the same name: Gershom. That I fell, bass-ackwards, into becoming Gershom Holder's Guardian Angel is quite another story. I will get to that later. But first, let me tell you about my lifelong relationship with Artemisia Gershom.

—

2

As I said, it was done in the old way, with the Creation Director commanding me to fulfill Guardian Angelic duties to a human being, from the very moment of birth until the last breath taken on the way to The World To Come.

Artemisia's mother wrote to her husband, who was then a man-child soldier, thrusted at random, for the duration, into the European Theatre of war. The newlyweds would need to communicate by letters for almost two years. He would serve in the war for six years, a warrior, but not protected by gleaming body armor. A Pilot, but not a commissioned officer. A teenager, though not allowed his own nascent rebellious youth. Broken, bound at every angle, held fast, tied up, bound at brain and heart. Not able to unify his own body, heart, brain, or guts, to discover his own singularity. Flight Sergeant Gershom was split and targeted, a stranger in a strange land, unfamiliar with even a notion of his own potential. Then he decided to get married.

The sexy part of war, immanent danger sparked by wild desire. It was war: the heart has . . . the heart had . . . its reasons.

Artemisia was about to be born, to become a stranger in a strange land; to join two other strangers in that strange land — her own mother and her own father, Gershoms all — each one of them destined to be *a stranger there.*

Her mother wrote to her brand-new husband. Her letters floated off into unknown destinations. The prediction is that her pregnancy will result in twins.

3

April 1945

Dearest,

I've just been to the doctors' — my first visit since I've been home, as the doctor had to take a week off. Dr. Spaulding is a woman doctor and is excellent. She took care of my grandmother, my mother, and my younger brother — so this will make the fourth generation in our family she has had. She is quite sure the baby will come in September—the Navy doctor had thought October. . . She has a hospital in Van Nuys at her disposal so that is good too considering how hard it is to get such facilities now. She will give me the best of care — so don't worry at all . . . She said there is a good chance that it will be twins . . . because of its size at this time, she believes that it could be twins.

4

So my artist is predicted to be born as a twin.

She was to be born during the mid-20th Century, during one of its wars. As her mother labored, as women have done since the unfortunate encounter with the Tree of Knowledge and that snake, I was called forth by our Creation Director to become the Guardian Angel of one of the expected twins. We Guardian Angels were still working in the medieval ways of guardianship. Get an instruction from on high. Go to it. Return for further instructions. Climb up and down our ladders.

I sensed that my job was very near. This task would turn out to be the guardianship for a human being who would have a very long lifetime. In fact, she is still alive today. She is now a woman of very great years, living well into this new age of the Gig Economy. She has made a successful transition into it in fact. I take no small credit for this.

But first, her birth.

5

Since it was suspected that she would be born as a twin, her mother was confined to bed during the last three months of her pregnancy. The Creation Director had selected me to be Guardian Angel for one of the expected twins. When I arrived at the birthing suite, I was joined by a colleague of mine, another Guardian Angel and we approached one another. With trembling recognition, we acknowledged, with reverent wings folded, that each one of us would be responsible for one of the twins as they inhaled into their new lungs their first breaths as individual human souls.

I went immediately to one side of the bed of the laboring mother. My compatriot, went to the other side. Together we would wait and could immediately spring into action at the first breaths of ensoulment of each of the twins. In addition, the laboring mother had her own Guardian Angel at the head of the bed, so that made three of us who were deeply immersed in the well-being of the mother and of each of her expected twins. And, in addition to us, there were several other Guardian Angels — for the doctor, her assistants, and for the nurses. It was quite a gathering, an unruly crowd, I could see.

That's the moment I started to think about making changes in methodology for the duties of Guardian Angels. This event stirred in me the concept of Guardian Angels working independently of the need for consultations with the Creation Director. As it was on that birth day, there was much to-ing and fro-ing among my peers to get instructions from the Creation Director. It was an unholy mess. It was chaos.

There was much confusion in the delivery suite as well as an intense aura of sadness and much fear emanating from the mother. The mother was alone in her world of birthing because the father was very far away and in grave mortal danger. He was immersed in a war of the world, which, at any moment, could kill him. I wanted to comfort the mother with my foreknowledge of his survival. But of course, in those days, I needed to get permission to act upon my proposed intercession and I needed to get it from the Creation Director. Permission was needed for me to act upon my wish to comfort the laboring mother. I hurried back up one of those ladders to the Creation Director's realm to obtain my official permission to do so.

While I was on this errand, there was intense confusion in the delivery room. An infant had come forward into our earthly domain and its Guardian Angel was near to him to begin presiding over his soul. But something was wrong. This infant was very still and silent and it was evident that he was severely damaged. The infant floated, hovering above us, as it took its first breath of earthly air. This breath would turn out to be the single and only breath it could manage. Enough, however, to provide a mere pinprick of an opening to accommodate its ensoulment. Yet all was not well.

My colleague, Guardian Angel to this firstborn, was grieving yet still attentive to the needs of his soul. Standing near him as he was lying on a stainless steel table being examined by three doctors and a nurse — each of these with their respective Guardian Angels — my colleague noted that this soul had inhaled a single breath into his damaged lungs. As such he was alive at birth and was an ensouled human being. My colleague's Guardian Angelic duties were not yet complete. She had witnessed that he had inhaled ensoulment and thus required her, as his Guardian Angel, to stand by until, or unless, he exhaled what might turn out to be his last breath. Her intense connection with this infant was utterly concentrated and deeply admirable.

Meanwhile, the second infant presented herself. Her brother and companion in the womb, had vanished. And, of course, she could not have known what was going on with her twin as she yet lacked comprehension of complicated human events. She was now alone. She had only vague and unformed gut feelings that something was wrong. I felt that this anxiety in her was my fault entirely. With my need to get permission from the Creation Director to instigate a comforting nudge to the laboring mother, I had not been available to assist the firstborn's Guardian Angel.

But the complex choreography of this multiple birth, combined with my self-motivated concept of how I could comfort the mother, had caused me to be absent for the moment of birth of the firstborn twin. That needed to change. I took note of those old ways and I vowed to the heavens that some day I would work to change the entire management of guardianship. There had to be a better way. Who said that Guardian Angels cannot multi-task?

Meanwhile, a sorrowful pantomime was taking place in the delivery suite. The doctor, a woman, which was unusual in those times, was speaking low and with very great tenderness into the ear of the partially anesthetized and still laboring mother:

> *"It was a boy. It was born undeveloped.*
> *He did not have strong lungs. Your other baby still seems viable. I can hear her very strong heartbeat. Abide, my dear. It will soon be here for you to have*

and to hold."

I noted that the other infant's Guardian Angel was still hovering gently and whispering to the wounded and malformed infant where he lay, utterly silent and very still. But what went perhaps unnoticed by the medical staff, was that this infant had inhaled a single breath upon his birth. And, as such, he was ensouled. And so his Guardian Angel was entrusted with whatever remaining life he had until he exhaled if or when he died. Thus, he still had his Guardian Angel during his last few seconds in the earthly realm.

She was reciting words to him as he approached The World to Come:

"You have a Guardian Angel."

His tiny face did reflect the flicker of light from his own Guardian Angel and his tightly closed eyelids did flutter with a golden refraction from her. She repeated into his ear:

"You have a Guardian Angel."

And for a moment this infant tapped into his own nascent, yet rapidly fading, humanity, in what was to be his own brief personhood. Although he was without language, he spoke to his Guardian Angel to let her know that:

"Yes. I do."

And his Guardian Angel whispered again, this time using a language that none will know until it is revealed at the end of a soul's embodiment. The boy died but, yes, during his last and his single exhalation of worldly breath, he heard his Guardian Angel whisper:

"You have had a Guardian Angel."

And he responded:

"Yes. I have."

The second twin was born, heavy and vigorous, and the weary mother was strong enough to hold and to speak clearly to her daughter:

> "Artemisia you will be, named after a famous artist. Like her, you will be strong and tenacious and fearless for every minute of whatever life you have. And you will have *art* in your name for the remainder of your entire life."

Artemisia would be one of two artists I would eventually be Guardian Angel for. Another artist. What a coincidence? Well, there are no such things as coincidences. Right? Co-incidence is simply one of the well-worn tools in a Guardian Angel's tool kit. Or should I say, in our Gig Guardian Angel Portfolio. And, as if to disprove the point that Guardian Angels cannot multi-task, I took on both of my charges with equal vigor and dedication. But the birth of my charge, Artemisia Gershom, and the sad departure of her twin, all of this in a crowded delivery suite, demonstrated to me that there had to be a better way to be a Guardian Angel in this complex world of human and divine interaction.

5

A few days after the birth of Artemisia, her mother

wrote a longer letter and sent it into the maw of war:

November, 1945

"My Darling,

I arrived at the hospital about 1: 45 A.M. and the baby was born at 8:01 A.M. When I went, I thought sure it would take longer than that as labor hadn't even started at that time — but it came on suddenly about 3:00 (I think) and they took me into the delivery room about 5:15 and the doctor got there about 5:45. She had to rush down as they hadn't expected it to happen so soon. And from 6:20 (there was a clock in the room which I looked at every time I could) to about 7:30 I don't remember very much except I was under ether most of the time and naturally couldn't feel everything but enough so I knew what the doctor was telling me to do and also enough so I was glad someone had invented ether. Then from about 7:30 to about 8:02 it was more like a dream with sound effects and some sensation but I couldn't see as the mask was over my face. All through the whole thing I felt I wanted to hurry as much as I could — a couple of times I almost automatically asked the nurse how much longer it would be. It was a strange sensation — I would vaguely think — then I would hear myself talking, as if it were someone else in another room. In fact, a rather funny thing happened — a woman in the next room had a little boy about half an hour before my baby came — I could hear her doctor or someone say it was a boy and I thought it was mine and I felt glad it was over — then I suddenly realized that it wasn't over. After that I kind of went out again I guess to sleep. I don't know — it was like a dream again — and the next thing I was aware of was a baby crying—just a little at first and the doctor saying "come on now, come on" then the mask was lifted up a little and I raised my head just a little and saw the baby lying on a table with a couple of nurses working over her. I really felt relieved then. I have more to write, but am feeling tired more. More for later!

I Love You,
XXXX from me
xxxx from baby

6

Whether, and what exactly, Artemisia's mother remembered during her moments in childbirth, it is impossible to know. In those days some laboring mothers were put under the influence of a drug with the nickname of Twilight Sleep and so she was not a very sharp witness for the events of her own labor. Over the years, when she spoke to Artemisia about her birth, she would repeat her impression that at one point she thought the birthing was over and that she heard someone say: "It was a boy" and then she was surprised that her labor continued, and when she came around for the second time someone said: "It's a girl." Her recollection never wavered.

Chava

1

That was a poignant and dramatic story. For a moment, I am without words. I am marveling at the genesis of Hannah-Naomi's new ideas about how Guardian Angels should do their work.

Hannah-Naomi, you seem to be very confident that you have come up with a new way to work in this world — using your own Freewill, making your own decisions, and multi-tasking, all without needing to consult with the Creation Director. You provide life-saving simultaneities and subtle nudges not unlike that small still voice inside a human being's mind and you bring into clear focus old memories so that a human being finally **gets** the impact of past events.

I note that Hannah-Naomi preens a bit, a small flutter of her wings, a bit of a smile. She is kvelling. Then, companionable, like a pal, she leans forward, offering me her rumpled pack of Camels. I wave them away, but say to her as I hand her a paint can lid for an ashtray:

"Go ahead. I mean, what's it going to do? Kill you?"

With a flick of a spark to her cigarette, Hannah-Naomi shifts a bit on my sofa pillows and continues.

Hannah-Naomi

1

As with Artemisia's birth, where her mother's recollection never wavered, so too did her mother's loving belief never waver — that Artemisia had been born as an artist. It is said that artists are born rather than made. Yet, even those so born need support and guidance, or might I also suggest the artist-born may require the occasional nudge from a Guardian Angel. I credit most of the reinforcement of Artemisia's artist-soul to her mother.

2

It may have started with a fire when Artemisia was five. The electric blanket on Artemisia's bed sparked and started to burn. At first it smoldered under the covers and gradually burrowed down into the mattress. Artemisia's mother woke up standing beside the burning mattress. In her arms was Artemisia. She did not know how she got there, standing before the flames, holding, safe and firm, her beloved child. In the morning she noted that Artemisia was unusually silent and withdrawn. Since her mother was an elementary school teacher, she decided to take Artemisia to her own school instead of sending Artemisia to her school.

After class, the kindergarten teacher came up to Artemisia's mother:

"You must come and see what Artemisia has made."

They went into the kindergarten classroom and over to the art corner where the easels and paints were. There, in bright tempera paint, on big sheets of newsprint, were many pictures; all red and orange and yellow, the paintings were of beds aflame. The kindergarten teacher said:

"Artemisia kept busy all afternoon making these pictures. She did not speak about the fire. She barely would speak to me while she worked. I let her do as she pleased. I believe that she used art to express her experience of the mattress fire."

That may have been the first time in Artemisia's life that she, quite literally, drew upon a pivotal experience of her life.

3

As the years sped by, Artemisia drew and painted many pictures, illustrations of events or things that she could not, or would not, speak about. When she was in the sixth grade and the kids were all invited to work on a class art project, Artemisia was tasked by their teacher to draw the Indians on the mural.

When Artemisia was in junior high school, her mother started to paint with oil paints during the Easter vacation week. At first she painted hills and trees and later she splurged on a large canvas for a landscape. For this project she purchased a small wooden case with a leather handle and two brass snap locks. In it resided a complete set of oil paints, the rainbow of colors plus turpentine, linseed oil, and three stiff bristle brushes. After a few days during that vacation, she brought her painting in to show Artemisia. It was a nice landscape of rolling green hillsides and blue sky with clouds.

Artemisia asked if she too could use some of the oil paints and make her own painting. And, of course, her mother was happy to loan her a few of her painting things to Artemisia. After an hour or so, Artemisia yelled for her mother to come in and see her painting. She had copied a photograph from a magazine for her painting — a bullfighter in a spangled costume and a twirling dusty bull. Her mother looked long and carefully at Artemisia's copy of the photograph. Artemisia was chattering away, excited by working with the new grownup medium of oil paints. Her mother turned away:

"Wait here for a second, Artemisia. I've got to go get something."

She returned in a few minutes with the paintbox, the several brushes, the two small bottles of turpentine and linseed oil, and three small brand-new blank canvasses.

"Here, these are for you, Artemisia. Don't forget to put down some newspapers when you work on these canvasses. Oil paints can splash a bit."

Her mother never painted another picture.

Now, while this seems like a sacrifice by a loving mother, it was also a gift of confidence for Artemisia's burgeoning artist soul. To bud, to sprout, to shoot forth, that was the gift of life that came from Artemisia's mother. She had given birth to this girlchild then given birth again — to the paintbox, the tubes of cerulean blue and of alizarin crimson and of titanium white, and to the small bottles of medium. She presented this treasure to Artemisia so that she could use these things to draw out further her own budding life. If Artemisia's mother had said to her upon presenting this new gift of life, "You have a Guardian Angel," I did not hear it. I was already too busy with Artemisia's guardianship and unable, as yet, to multi-task.

Chava

1

But you saw these events in Artemisia's life. Saw them as they unfolded from her birthing forward. I would guess that perhaps you were there on the sidelines, nudging your charge, and maybe giving a little bit of a nudge for Artemisia's mother also, urging her to give the paint-box to Artemisia. Yes?

You paint a picture of perhaps many moments in Artemisia's growing up that nudged her toward being an artist. Including and most importantly, her own mother's influences on her. Isn't it true that a mother's influence upon a daughter can be instrumental in how a girl turns out as an adult?

I would also guess that since you were still working with the Creation Director in the old-fashioned way with Artemisia, that you might have been further motivated as Artemisia grew. As you worked in guardianship with Artemisia over the years, you, yourself Hannah-Naomi, may have begun to visualize new ways to do the work of a Guardian Angel.

Hannah-Naomi

1

There is even more to my story. And, yes Chava, you have noted that, as my charge was growing up, I could see many other ways I could work with her, especially if I became more independent and used more of my own Freewill.

By way of background, I will review for you my meeting with the Creation Director after I had developed new ways of working as a Gig Guardian Angel. As I sat across the desk from the Creation Director, I asked permission, in the old way, if I could smoke.

"Mind if I . . ."

"Go ahead, Hannah-Naomi. What's it going to do? Kill you?"

There it is again: I hear this all the time. As you may recall: Guardian Angels do not die.

—

2

And how did I contact the Creation Director to request this meeting? Why, email! Of course:

From: Guardian Angel Hannah-Naomi

To: Creation Director

Subject: IMPORTANT ANNOUNCEMENT

ATTENTION ALL HEAVENLY HOSTS AND CREATION DIRECTOR

It's time to change millennia of notions about Guardian Angels.

It's time to change how we work in this new Gig Economy.

Now's the time for BOLD NEW ACTION. NO MORE OF THE NONSENSE THAT SAYS:

Angels have no Freewill. Angels cannot multi-task.

THERE'S A BETTER WAY

LET'S TALK!!

STAY TUNED

BE THERE!!!

Yours still truly: Guardian Angel Hannah-Naomi, President, Gig Guardian Angels, LLC

You like, Chava? I can do ads online. Some might see it as spam. I see it as a quick method for: ATTENTION GETTING ADVERTISING.

Anyway, it works. I got the attention of a very busy individual, our Creation Director.

3

And there I sat across the massive, if not profoundly disheveled, Creation Director's desk. I was ready with my proposals.

As for desks, it was surprisingly untidy considering whose desk this is — the desk of the Divine, big D. It was stacked, although stacked implies some heavenly form of order — with all due respect — there was no discernable order at that desk. It is, rather, slung and strewn with ragged file folders, creased world maps, wadded candy wrappers, coffee-stained paper cups — paper? For the Creation Director? Also there are old chewed-up and useless ball point pens. Ballpoint pens? Oily wires and parts of wounded angel wings protrude from a place for everything and everything in its place. Now, to accommodate my Camel, the Creation Director pushes toward me, across the divine accumulation of this busy chief executive's desk, a small glass dish with the words imprinted on it: *Los Angeles Angelus Bar*.

Reinforced by my fresh cigarette, I begin, undaunted, my presentation to the Creation Director:

—

4

First, if I may say so Creation Director: many wise and learned scholars, from a variety of religious backgrounds, include references about Angels and Angelology in their writings. There are opinions and commentary galore about the nature and origins of Guardian Angels. There are so many very definitive entries on the topic. For example:

Angels may take no action without a command from You, the Creation Director.

Angels walk upright.

Speak Hebrew.

Can fly in the air.

Can foretell the future.

Angels may take the shape of human beings or of animals.

Please make note of this last, if you will Creation Director. I continue:

Angels have no evil intentions

Some righteous human beings could even be transformed into angels.

Angels are not perfect.

Human beings may call upon angels for help.

Every living thing gets a message from a Guardian Angel: To Live!

Angels have no Freewill.

Angels cannot multi-task.

The Creation Director nods, leans back in the somewhat shopworn supernal throne, gestures impatiently with a circulating first finger, urging me to speed it up, and I do:

So many sure things are written about angels. Yes, Creation Director?

Chava

1

I can't believe I am listening to Hannah-Naomi's disquisition. Here I am, sitting here in my own studio — there is rain pounding at my skylights, right now, and I am listening to a real live Guardian Angel. Well, if she is, indeed, alive, really. She seems to be. She is sitting on my sofa. Now she is clutching to her chest one of my sofa cushions as she speaks.

But maybe I am hallucinating. What if I am hallucinating? Maybe I have finally gone round the bend and this is all just an elaborate and dramatic case of senile dementia. I am seventy-five after all. A lot can happen at our age. But Hannah-Naomi looks and acts real to me. And I do always appreciate a well-researched piece of work. Hannah-Naomi is nothing if not her own kind of scholar. We're having a back-and-forth conversation, well, me mostly listening. This is a process of discovery for me, living here in the diaspora of the secular, asking Hannah-Naomi how things may work in this complicated, tangled earthly and Divine Domaine, big D. In a way, this is not unlike the ancient rabbis and their Responsa. I ask Hannah-Naomi about something and she responds to my questions. And here she is again: standing right here in my studio, standing in a slanting beam of morning sunlight that has just broken through the storm clouds. Hannah-Naomi enlightens me just as the sun enlightens this studio. She picks up on her presentation to the Creation Director:

Hannah-Naomi

1

My audience with the Creation Director continued:

What I am here for today, is to discuss Freewill in Guardian Angels. Mine, as well as pending Freewill among the entire universe of Guardian Angelhood.

Times have changed. A new Gig Economy is upon us. Now it's up to us to change how our jobs — which I now refer to as *gigs* — are conducted and also how our responsibilities of guardianship shall be streamlined and brought up to date in this digital, this increasingly complex universe. This new era, the Gig Economy, will change every human and angelic life. Are you willing to hear my proposal Creation Director?

The Creation Director nods a go-ahead, although there is a sense of strain between us now. To drive home my additional points, I speed up the presentation:

I am specifically requesting of you that the following

traditional aspects of the job of Guardian Angel be changed to suit this new era. In summary, our old traditional ways include these:

One — Angels may take shape of human beings or of animals.

Two — Some righteous human beings may be transformed into angels.

Three — Angels may take no action without a command from the Creation Director.

Four — Angels have no Freewill .

Five — Angels cannot multi-task.

These things must change. Point three, most urgently, needs to change. I am here to demonstrate that, I myself, do have indeed, Freewill. I myself am already the embodiment of some of these changes which are as follows:

I have already been able to take action without a command from you, the Creation Director.

I have already, by my recent actions, demonstrated that I do have Freewill .

And, this last, I have already demonstrated, on a daily basis, moment-to-moment, even, my ability to multi-task, even this I can now do quite well, thank you very much.

There is an icy silence from the Creation Director. An apocalyptic silence. Well, no surprise that. The Creation Director is deft in a display of apocalypticisms.

Well. Well.

Chava

1

Well, on Hannah-Naomi's first point: I am truly convinced. I have seen with my own eyes and open heart, many human beings who have become angels. I have not needed Hannah-Naomi to convince me on that point. From the pens of many learned scholars, in their learned theses, I note that we are assured that some righteous human beings may be transformed into angels. With immense grief, I can see it for myself.

Are these human beings not righteous? Are these two human beings not angels? The heart breaks. Their wounded aching hearts reach out with human arms to comfort gentle, frightened creatures: a dog and a cat. These animals cling to these angelic beings. For Protection. Solace. Endurance. These human beings do the right thing. They cherish these creatures. Swoop them up. Embrace them. Remove them from extreme danger and provide shelter and food. It is the right thing to do by two righteous human souls. In moments like these — cherished blessings seen in their millions on icy computer screens at 3:30 A.M. or, horrifying, viewed in person, after vicious bombs have already claimed their bullseyes — two righteous human beings step up and are, instantly, unequivocally, transformed into angels.

Hannah-Naomi

1

I NEED TO CONTINUE MY CASE with the Creation Director, who blurts out in apparent exasperation:

"You certainly do have the chutzpah, Hannah-Naomi."

It is not a prescient act of mind-reading for me to know that the Creation Director is displeased. I feel waves of wrath emanating from across the desk, aimed at me. I'm in for it now.

"You have the nerve, Hannah-Naomi, to seek to circumvent my leadership, my orders, as the one who has been, and will be forevermore, Director of all Creation. I manage all Guardian Angels. It is my job. My responsibility. Only I can do this thing."

The supernal throne, creeks a bit.

The Creation Director is fuming, rather grandly, actually. A storm, heaven-sent, with lightening bolts and thunderous crashes dislodges my hair clips. Some of them clatter to the floor.

"Surely you know what a risk you take — thou blasphemer — you with your faith in the Gig Economy which you seem to hold, now, as holy."

I am undaunted by this accusation from my Creation Director. Blasphemer? Me? I hastily continue:

Might I add, Creation Director, meaning no disrespect, the many attributes of Guardian Angels as related in the works of scholars from many spiritual orientations? I want to note here, Creation Director, that from Anglicanism to Zoroastrianism, every major and many minor religions have explored Guardian Angelship. Whether believers or not, great minds of all sorts have addressed Guardian Angelic qualities, attributes, even negative aspects. There is much literature available on the topic of Guardian Angelology.

So many sure things are written about angels. Yes Creation Director? And so many attributes and certainties. And I must note this peculiar conclusion and it is this: whether a learned scholar comes out on the side of believing in angels or of NOT believing, said scholar is very confident of either opinion. How, I ask, how can this be so? You see what I mean?"

The Creation Director nods, glancing away from my intensity. I continue, speeding up my words, racing to make further points:

There are definite opinions on both sides of the question: Do you believe in Guardian Angels or not? And loads of supporting material to rationalize either stance. I conclude that the topic is of very great interest from proponents or from opponents, of either side. Why? I could ask — how come someone who does NOT believe in angels would spend so much time rationalizing that stance? Isn't that akin to proving a negative? Isn't that considered to be impossible? And why bother? If one does not believe, why go to all that trouble?

2

Now this footnote, which I discovered in the *Encyclopaedia Judaica*, is of particular interest to me: more than simply a note for a foot, I see the following statement as a note for the head, for the brain, for our accretions of common sense based on eons of being Guardian Angels. So, listen up. Take heed, a word to the wise:

> *"The modern Jewish attitude to angels tends to regard the traditional references and descriptions as symbolic, poetic, or representing an earlier world-concept. Contemporary movements such as Reform Judaism and certain sections of the Conservative Movement have either completely expunged from the liturgy all references to angels or, where they remain, have understood them in poetic or mythological terms. They feel that a belief in their existence is out of keeping with a modern approach to the world and to the belief in a monotheistic God and cannot be reconciled with modern rationalism."*

Pay heed, I beg of you Creation Director, to how this statement sounds very controlling — both to Guardian Angels and to human beings who might be tempted to believe that, yes, there are such beings as Guardian Angels.

I am met by the Creation Director's most intent and unblinking divine stare.

Note if you will, Creation Director, the tone of urgency in the use of the word *expunged*. Why so urgent? Why should references mentioned in holy and revered scripture, in an encyclopedia no less, be expunged?

3

I suggest that the human beings — scholars, philosophers, commentators — that were responsible for those powerful concepts were trying to control what other human beings would think about Guardian Angels. It sounds to me like the very idea of belief in angels could be in conflict with the belief in monotheism, as per the *Encyclopaedia Judaic*a.

Am I right Creation Director?

I crave a fresh Camel. I stick one to my lower lip. A thin shaft of smoke drifts upward into my eyes. I squint as I puff into the air that refreshing first breath.

Am I right?

The Creation Director reaches across the desk, gesturing, fingertips flapping impatiently at my pack of Camels and asks:

"May I?"

I shake the pack in the direction of the Creation Director and a few Camels poke out over the top.

I mean all of this: With all due respect, Creation Director. Now, my next point is key to being a Gig Guardian Angel:

4

We have, for eons, had to keep checking back and forth with the Creation Director — to yourself — to get permission to do this or that act. It was very time consuming and, well, oftentimes it was simply an unnecessary additional step during a complicated process that only the operative Guardian Angel understood. Very inconvenient to be hustling up and down ladders, up and down from the Creation Director, in need of obtaining further instructions for our work. It was rumored, indeed written about, that we had no Freewill. No ability for self-determination.

It's a lot, I know. I let it sink in for a moment, then, as the Creation Director blows out a puff of blue smoke overhead, I continue:

To wrest control from Guardian Angels and to set a dialog going among human beings to delegitimize Guardian Angels.That has apparently been the goal of some scholars from our own and from several other belief systems.

See what I'm saying here, Creation Director?

Not to mention there exist very definitive opinions

about Guardian Angels like these two, in particular, posited by a very learned scholar:

"Angels cannot multi-task. Angels have no Freewill."

I must interrupt with my fantasy: How do you, oh wise and learned scholar, how do you know that? How do you know whether or not Angels can multi-task?

How could an otherwise wise scholar say such bold and definite things about angels when — after all, let's face it— nobody among these earthbound scholars had ever seen, nevermind sat down with, to have a head-to-head discussion with, any of us genuine Guardian Angels? Right? I ask you.

The magnificence of the Creation Director's first puff on that Camel is, truly, Fabulous, big F. Yet again, the Creation Director has absolute command of impressive flares of effects that may some day enter legend. The Creation Director turns the lighted end of the cigarette and stares at its glowing ember appreciatively, like a long-lost love, and sighs deeply. Apparently it has been a very long time since the last one.

Taking this moment, I inject:

I stand before — or, in this case, am seated before you — as the personification of a Guardian Angel who has abundant Freewill and who can, and does, often multi-task.

There is a deep sigh from across the Creation Director's desk accompanied by an enormous — might I say, legendary? — puff of blue smoke.

"Are we finished here, Hannah-Naomi?"

—

5

Now the Creation Director speaks to me:

"All right, then, Hannah-Naomi. I have listened to your presentation. I have heard your voice. And, reluctantly, I agree with you on some salient points. Your thinking even demonstrates much in the way of Freewill in Guardian Angels and thus you prove, and enhance even, some of your very own points. You are the very embodiment — if you don't mind my putting it like this — of Guardian Angels. Plus, you are both creative and scholarly, if I do not exaggerate, and this will serve you well in your new angelic enterprise.

"Tell you what I am going to do. I have stipulations mind you. I have two of them:

"One: We will allow you to make your presentation to the other angels in my employ, under the condition that, at the completion of your examples of Gig Guardian Angels that you allow them to decide for themselves whether or not to join your company. Note the concept of *deciding for themselves.* As you see, I am allowing that angels, some angels, perhaps only Guardian Angels, can act with some aspects of Freewill. Not all angels. I must emphasize that. If your presentation is convincing to even one single other Guardian Angel in the room, then that angel will be free to join your enterprise. But you must be willing to accept that perhaps none of the Guardian Angels in my employ would chose to join you thus."

I nod.

"Two: You will meet with me from time to time for a progress report. I will want a full accounting of what you have done — or not been able to do — and you and I will meet in a place and at a time that works for both of us. I know you will be busy. I am too. But make time, or mark my words, I will withdraw my support for your new Gig Guardian Angel enterprise. Is that clear? "

I nod again and say: abundantly.

"You are confident, then, Hannah-Naomi?"

Again I respond: abundantly.

"Well then go and sin no more."

This sounds a bit off to me: You don't mean that do you Creation Director?

"Oh, well no. These stock phrases, slogans, tag lines, modern slang, bits and pieces of scripture — they stick like glue. Go, I say. Go and do what you are bound to do, Hannah-Naomi."

I rise and unfold my wings: right, will do.

Then, leaning across the table, the Creation Director gestures and in a confidential tone says to me:

"One more small thing, Hannah-Naomi. As a personal favor to me, could you be an angel and keep me supplied with more of these heavenly Camels?"

Chava

1

WHEW! I am worn out. As with study of many ethical concepts in scripture, I am torn back and forth as one argument is tested against another and yet another. My head swims with *compare and contrast* of differing points of view. Hannah-Naomi is nothing if not well-read. It is obvious that she has studied, stored, and recorded masses of information about Guardian Angels. And for that, I would praise her. Yet, I am exhausted. I am not sure if I understand or can comprehend all of her points. I am also impressed with her fearlessness in addressing her Creation Director. At this point I must agree that Hannah-Naomi has a super-abundance of Freewill. She's not shy; I give her that. But where to go with all of this? She claims to be an independent Gig Guardian Angel. Her confidence begs the question: But how does this new Gig Economy work for guardianship responsibilities in Guardian Angels?

Can you tell me more about that, Hannah-Naomi?

Hannah-Naomi

1

First, I shall demonstrate memory work. Let's see how long and old memories have affected one of my charges:

Gershom Holder remembers when he and his parents flew all over the place in their own Cessna. The summer when Gershom turned eleven, they decided to fly from California to Florida. And back.

Gershom's father, The Pilot, had a cap, a flying talisman perhaps, a picturesquely beat up, somewhat threadbare black wool baseball-style hat. The bill of this cap had been folded so many times, jammed into so many pants pockets, tugged at so diligently, that all of the stiffness had gone out of it. At the crown of this cap there was a permanent crease extending from what would be eartop to eartop. The underside of the bill — which at one time might have been yellow — was now a grubby beige. It had faded black letters on it reading: HOLD. That had been The Pilot's moniker in the Royal Air Force where he had served throughout the war in Europe. He was inducted into the service when he was nineteen and would be de-mobilized six years later. For him, parts of that war never ended. He would never forget, and continued to feel, that he would forever be — The Pilot.

After the war, the former RAF Pilot had had to obtain a private pilot's license in the San Fernando Valley before he could pilot his own little Cessna. A bit of a comedown, a humiliation for him, perhaps. But nevermind. California after his war had been, for him, a strange land and he, the stranger in it. Taking flight lessons from these crop-dusting, rough-riding pilots, had been almost surrealistic for him. The Pilot endured the surprisingly simplistic civilian flying instructions and aced every single maneuver and solo flight and received his private pilot's license in record time.

2

The Cessna he had purchased was tied down out at a little ragtag air field in the San Fernando Valley, Coffin Field. It had a more formal name, but The Pilots who tied down out there all referred to it as Coffin Field in honor of the man who ran the place: Hank Coffin. Nice name for the manager of a small airfield with its gravel tie downs for a population of civilian private pilots and their planes: Cessnas, Stinsons, Aeroncas, and Beechcraft. Hank was an old school, crop dusting pilot, more dust than crop in those days. Hanky, his nickname, was a jovial red-faced type. It's a good idea to be jovial when your last name is Coffin and you oversee about twenty-five civilian aircraft tie-downs, an aviation gas pump, and two slumping aircraft hangars. Hanky presides over his flying kingdom from a low-roofed, ratty flight shack. Behind his desk, piloting his domain, he teeters backward on a murderously defective swivel chair. The screeching back and arms of this wreck tilt so far back that Hanky looks like he might launch straight upward into the clouds of the nicotine-smoked ceiling. His desk was stacked — although *stacked* implies some form of order — there was none at that desk — it was, rather, slung and strewn with ragged flight plan folders, creased aviator's maps, wadded candy wrappers, coffee-stained paper cups, aged and reeking cigarette butts, chewed up and useless ball point pens, oily wires and engine parts; a place for everything and everything in its place. Hanky presides, godlike, over his Domaine. Big D.

Gershom can still picture, and will forever remember, the air strip. The gravel is just about adequately paved right down the middle, a narrow runway, lining up, dead-reckoning, with three towering smoke stacks next to the garbage facility serving much of the San Fernando Valley. At takeoff, the little planes, navigated by their weekend pilots, have to roar up the field with as much power under the cowling as pilot and craft can muster and take a slight left tip of the wings just after the wheels leave the ground in order to clear, barely, and at an odd angle, the smokestacks. Gershom can look down and clearly see the insides of those smokestacks, burning red with ample combustible trash provided by the citizens of the San Fernando Valley. He loved that crazy takeoff.

3

On some days, the little Cessna is grounded for minor repairs and general maintenance. Today, The Pilot scrunches along on his back with his head heading downhill inside the echoing metal skin of this Cessna's tail-dragger fuselage. He is headed down there to adjust the ailerons. Or something. Meanwhile, Gershom is tasked with scouring the tarmac for stray nuts, bolts, and screws. He collects these in a jar and turns them in to The Pilot when he's done with his work. Gershom's mother takes flying lessons every weekend so that there will always be two pilots on board during flight. The itinerary for the flight from California to Florida and back again required several months of flying lessons for Gershom's mother.

At Coffin Field there are two enormous beat-up airplanes, looming, dented hulks with cartoons of livid snarling sharks painted onto their nose sections. These battered craft are, of course, relics of The Pilot's war: retired fighters from the Flying Tiger Squadron. The sides are pocked and dented and the planes squat, sinking into squashy balding tires. Alongside the shark teeth are painted figures and slogans: a side view of a naked lady with big bazooms and tiny pink lace panties along with the words, *Bombs Away Baby!*

Gershom is not really clear on when or where those old planes flew or in what war. It must have been a war. The planes are snarling. It will be many years later before Gershom can identify the dates of the first atomic bombs and his own birthday, only a scant few days apart. Gershom was born two weeks after the first atom bombs were borne.

Gershom's family was not rich; owning and maintaining a little Cessna costs much less than owning and maintaining a new Chevy pickup. During the cross-country flight, inexpensive lodgings were always available, parking lot motels with little one story house-ettes, centered around brilliant turquoise chlorinated swimming pools.

4

The route cross country included Texas, Louisiana, Mississippi, then Florida, plus the reverse flight going west. They take off at dawn to avoid the hot thermals for a few hours before landing at the next destination. Afternoons are for touring around in each town and city. The little family wanders in public parks beneath huge trees that sag under hanging mosses. It is hot above the leaves and the gauze of the moss. Walking is labored and slow in the thick damp heat. Shafts of sunlight pierce the negative spaces between the leaves and branches making patterns on the melting sidewalks.

Throughout the tour of downtowns and city halls, there flutter many red flags with "X's" slashing thru them. California has a bear in the center of its flag. These red flags have a big "X" from hem to hem. As they wander around Mississippi and Louisiana, Gershom sees these things but he is unsure about whether or not he should be a bother and ask The Pilot about them.

In each of these foreign towns Gershom's family rides on local busses — destinations unknown — and they ride the whole route, all the way to the bus terminal and then, chatting with the next bus driver as he comes on duty, the bus rumbles all the way back to where they came from.

"Y'all folks don't sit back there."

The bus driver motions for them to move forward in his vehicle.

Along the way Gershom sees shacks made from crooked grey wood and skinny little kids and buckets, flung empty onto the ground, and ragged bony hens pecking dirt and old women in drooping flowered dresses and wood slats for stairs ascend crooked porches. On this bus tour, Gershom sits inside the bus and the driver, fat and authoritative, motions proprietarily for the family to look at this and to look at that, showing us his town.

It is memory, memory at work in Gershom. These memories were to become indelible.

From where he is, Gershom, sitting behind the bus driver, stares at the driver's fat red neck as it rolls over the back of his gray bus uniform collar and sees that his neck hairs are red and sprout from his red skin, shorn and prickly. Gershom looks out the bus window and sees big dusty trees, Nehigh Orange soda pop crates, rusted American Flyer wagons, and headless broken pink dolls. Everywhere there are pecking hens gleaning bugs.

Gershom wonders about the bus antennas, each one pierced with a row of metal objects—cones and spheres and cubes. These antennae are stuck onto the outside of the front window of each bus; cone, cone, sphere, or cube, cone, sphere. The bus driver bellows over his grinding gearbox and says that those cones and spheres are for "them folks who cain't read". Each different combination of cones and cubes and spheres indicates a street name.

Until this moment, Gershom has seen nothing outside of his own world of the San Fernando Valley's orange trees and dirt roads; nothing outside of little neighborhoods of brand new box tract houses and a scatter of brand new elementary schools, temporary classrooms made of pink stucco. These *temps,* as they are called, are set directly on top of fresh blacktop. But, strangely, the old houses in Mississippi don't look so very different to Gershom from the old houses alongside the dirt road farming acreage of the San Fernando Valley. And the old ladies in flowering dresses in Mississippi are not shaped much differently from Gershom's own grandma back home.

The little kids in the Mississippi front yards stare at the bus as it rolls along, arrogant and righteous and tut-tutting through their lives.

Tomorrow Louisiana, four days for Texas, skip across New Mexico, sleep in Arizona, then home to Coffin Field.

5

When Gershom's mother unlocks the back door to the kitchen, the house smells stuffy. It's been shut tight for two weeks, windows and doors locked.

Gershom dashes down the hall to check his room, then trots back again into the living room. Just a tad hyper, Gershom wants to debrief the flight, to explore, to question and to talk about all of the experiences and sights of that cross-country excursion and he chatters, breathless, babbling, pumped.

"Dad. Dad. Dad. What did you think those big X flags meant? What do you think those big Xs stood for? What did you think of that bus driver's guided tour? Did you see the kids with the broken wagons? Just like mine, huh, Dad? And what about those things on the busses for the people who couldn't read? Do you think there are grown-ups in Louisiana who can't read? And wasn't it hot and sticky down there? We're lucky we don't have that kind of weather, huh? Huh, Dad? Dad?"

Cranky, beat, The Pilot slumps into the davenport, flapping his flight cap on his knees.

"Dad. Dad. Dad, what did you think of those X flags? And the bus with the cubes and stuff? Dad. Dad?"

Methodical, The Pilot folds his cap into its habituated crease and places it with a little proprietary pat, onto the wide arm of the davenport.

"Get a grip, Ger."

6

Hot and still, the afternoon sun is stifled against the yellowing shades of the living room windows. Gershom's mother flips them up and they spin and snap, noisy, and she lifts the lower pane of each double hung window to let in air and sunshine.

As the sun streaks across the hardwood floors and a hot San Fernando Valley breeze lifts the curtain ruffles, Gershom's mother thinks to herself:

"We certainly do have a Guardian Angel."

7

Other memories will flood back to Gershom, even decades later.

With The Pilot and his mother as co-pilot, off they went into the wild blue yonder. Hundreds of times. Up, up and away. And during one flight, oil started oozing upwards from the cowls of the Cessna. It flowed, leisurely, upward on the windscreen, shoved by the wash of the propeller. The Pilot looked down onto the desert floor below and there was an old fashioned airstrip used for ranchers and the clumsy little airstrip had yuccas growing here and there and it had a big white X painted at one end which was to warn a pilot not to use that airstrip any more: danger, danger. The Pilot slowed the Cessna, drifted it downward, low and slow, almost in a stall, and deftly placed the landing gears onto the ground, weaving this way and that way between the yuccas and when the plane stopped, he shut down the engine and the propeller stopped, vertical in stillness, silent, and The Pilot opened the cockpit doors. "Run. Run as fast as you can. Run for about a football field away."

And you all ran, ran, ran as fast as you could to escape from the Cessna and you stood between your mother and father, looking back at the Cessna from where you were, about a hundred yards away, waiting for the airplane to blow up. As you watched, you saw the landscape around the makeshift landing strip, and you saw in the distance from the airstrip there was a round red form jutting up from the horizon line, way far out there. That would have been Cabezon. It was New Mexico desert with intensely blue skies and white magical boiling clouds that are flat and grey on the bottom and a stark single red peak stood up from the desert floor, and out there, miles away from this landing strip, out there in the middle of this wild blue yonder, in the middle of nowhere, there you three stood. Waiting. And you and The Pilot and your mother watched as the Cessna sat there about a football field in the distance. Still and silent, it was way out there. It sat there, the Cessna. Just sat there. And there it sat. Still sat, silent and still.

It did not blow up.

And remember coming home from that flight, Gershom? And the house was hot and stuffy and your mother flipped open the roller shades and lifted the window panes and the living room became bright and still. The Pilot folded his flight cap — his talisman with the word HOLD in fading marks on the underside of its bill. He placed it on the arm of the davenport with a pat. You were all home safe, Gershom, and your mother thought, but did not say out loud:

"We must have a Guardian Angel."

CHAVA

1

WHAT AN INTERESTING AND EXCITING LIFE your Gershom Holder had. And yet you said that you did not meet him until your original charge, Artemisia Gershom, was in college. They were both in college at the same time. I deduce, if I am correct, that you were not yet Gershom Holder's Guardian Angel back then?

Again, I am asking questions.

Again, I am disoriented and a bit confused by your relating to me some of Gershom's childhood memories.

I need help Hannah-Naomi.

HANNAH-NAOMI

1

AH YES, CHAVA. Sadly there is more. And you are correct to deduce that Gershom's childhood memories of long ago were much later induced by a nudge from me. Chimera? Perhaps. But look.

2

They flew all over the place. The Holders explored the whole country, state by state. Always they flew under the talisman of the black cap of The Pilot. Gershom loved those crazy take-offs. His mother loved their adventures, some of them narrow escapes from disaster, but they always returned home. And, thus, every time she flipped up the shades in their stuffy little house after two weeks of flying into the wild blue yonder, she breathed a sigh of relief with:

"Wow. We sure must have a Guardian Angel."

3

And then there was one disaster that they could not avoid. It would be a bumpy ride with Gershom's mother navigating her final solo flight. Veering this way and that way, tossed up and down by gusts into violent altitudes, the journey of her illness progressed downward — with tests, diagnoses, prognostications, treatments, supplications, prayers even. Raised hopes, dashed again, then slipping, slipping, will it be now? Or now? Or now? Gershom was twelve when his life tumbled down and downward as his mother's life crashed. And then she died.

And so soon, too soon, after his bewildering — no — after his devastating loss, Gershom was about to become a man standing before the grownups at his own Bar Mitzvah.

"Today, I am a man."

No. He was not. He was, still, a little boy. This is not to diminish Gershom Holder. But his mother's illness, then death, stunted something inside of him without his even being conscious of it at the time. How could he be conscious of being unconscious? Not being part of those life-and-death decisions, conducted between the oncologist and the beloved ones — the grown-ups — Gershom's mother had said:

"He is too young. We will make the decisions. We must protect him. Maybe he has a Guardian Angel."

And then she died. Gershom was twelve.

Then a few, a very few, months after the funeral, Gershom stands at the bimah for his Bar Mitzvah, ready or not, to make the affirmations about his new adulthood.

"Today, I am a man."

The faces in the room surround Gershom with love and pity, in too-human bumbling efforts to comfort him, to encourage and to embrace Gershom's struggling identity, from afar, way down there in their seats beneath the bimah. There was nothing they could do. Really nothing. Yet the adults, the grown-ups, so many of them mothers, seated down there in the seats below the bimah, all of them, were focused in mindful loving sympathy, and yet, speechless as courtesy requires, with beating hearts pumping Gershom up, it was hoped, by the mothers, so many mothers. Words fail. Words are carefully harvested in so many hearts. Words fail. No, not exactly. Words are extraneous to this moment, but are stored away, for later, perhaps.

"Today, I am a man."

Gershom sets off to make his speech:

> "Today I want to remember the six women in Torah who guided and supported Moses during the Exodus. They are: Yokheved, his mother; Miriam, Yokheved's daughter and Moses' elder sister; the Pharoah's daughter, Bitya; Tzippora, Moses' wife; and the fifth and sixth of these women, Shifra and Pua, midwives whom Pharaoh had tasked to kill every male Hebrew child. I stand here among you this day, as a Hebrew child."

—

The room shifts. Just a few feet shuffle on the floor beneath their seats. Gentle courtesy requires silence, but not in cold disapproval of this child, this lad. Gershom Holder, here for his Bar Mitzvah, needing the support and the kindness of strangers. The urgent kindness of strangers did suffer to communicate, in some way, their loving-kindness up to Gershom as he stood there alone on the bimah. They stirred, one or two of the mothers breathing silent tears.

"Today, I am a man. Today, I am . . ."

No. On that day Gershom was simply not a man. His pain exceeded what any man could endure, whether he were twenty-five, or fifty, or twelve years of age. He paused, speechless. Words failed. Whether it was Gershom who struggled or whether it was an adult, perhaps the rabbi herself, someone intervened with their human frailty of loving-kindness proffered, and Gershom was suddenly transported into a small room behind the bimah. It was not unlike a dream.

There were words and words, spoken around his ears, but nonetheless, incomprehensible. Gentle words of flustered kindness as several mothers, but not Gershom's mother, and as several fathers, including his own, tried to find words to comfort Gershom or to urge Gershom onward and, of course, failing, but give them credit for having gentle good intentions. These grown-ups offered to Gershom sincere forms of love, from their loving, if inadequate, hearts. Beautiful, beautiful boy.

"Today, I am a man."

Then Gershom's remaining parent, duty-bound to make of him a man this day, decides to assert manhood. The Pilot steps forward to turn and point his son away from the soft hum of the gentle choir of mothers and their serenade of comfort and loving-kindness. Then The Pilot says to Gershom, man to man:

"Get a grip, Ger."

Chava

1

So sad, Hannah-Naomi. This just breaks my heart. I do not like The Pilot. How could he have been so brutal? But still: his brutality was only words. Mere words. I would guess that Gershom could put them aside and get on with his life. Am I right, Hannah-Naomi?

So then, let's us move on too: you met Gershom Holder when he was in college with Artemisia Gershom? Is that right? How did that unfold?

Hannah-Naomi

1

The scene is mid-sixties, a party. The gathering consists of college students, art majors, all of them in this case.

For a wild party, it is not very wild. Well, sure enough, loud. Rock and Roll, all the favorites, full volume. *Blond on Blond*. The usual enhancements to music: munchies, a hookah, bubbling with each breath — breathe in, hold, hold, hold, blow out, puff. Joints swing from hand to hand, tiny red beacons helicoptering through the dark. Feed your head. The guests, cross-legged, on mattresses on the floor. Oh, for heaven's sake! Here in one room are assembled all of the expected accoutrements of their times. Clichés abound. These art students represent a Bohemian cluster of the innocents of that era, the intelligentsia of the naive.

My Guardian Angelic duties of that era were to protect and guide Artemisia Gershom from birth. Now in college, she was immersed in girlish lovelorn capitulation, mooning over one after another of the art students, or rather, artist wannabes. Her current very great love was Gershom Holder.

At this party, he is in love. He is always in love. Yet, he never lets on to anybody about his longings. Always in love.

Or out of it.

He was strident in protecting his aloofness: a real pro, making sure nobody would trespass his tee-shirt and Levi-clad self. Paint-splashed. Evocative. His costume supplied narration for who he was and what he did — or, rather, what he aspired to do, well, someday. Silent, squinting and inhaling his prop, the sizzling cigarette stub, he slurps a quick sip from his broken mug of dark and now-cold coffee; he had practiced his suggestive moves with paint cans and scumbling brushes. He was an Artist.

The nonchalance with which he dispersed his beauty — for he knew he was beautiful — enhanced his beauty. Made it somehow untouchable. Thus indifferent, he was always on display. Always desirable. He was ever indifferent to, yet a sly manipulator of, the glances of women. Men, too, I suppose. But it would be a very long time before that gaze could be mentioned. His power was inscrutable and he knew it. He dispensed it, drop by drop, just like cerulean blue on canvas.

With just a bit of prodding, the ineffable Guardian Angelic nudge, I made sure that Gershom noticed one of the female party guests — my very own charge, Artemisia Gershom. I made sure, with just a nudge, that he glanced in her direction, with unblinking careless seduction. And it was working.

Then I nudged Artemisia: Do something different. Something unexpected.

Thus nudged, she did so, or tried, rather:

She takes up her own paint brush, dips it deeply, suggestively swirling it, into a jar of cerulean blue, dives into that wild blue yonder and, without needing to even glance in the direction of Gershom she painted, suggestively, the trees and grasses of their plein air lesson. And Gershom lured his prey — Artemisia — with studied insouciance. He worked on his own painting, with measured caresses of paint brush on canvas, concentrating all the while on his effects upon Artemisia. With that obsessive stoned party-goer ogling him, Gershom ignored her, ignored as well anybody else who might also view him with hearts a-flutter. He was not original. But he was very good indeed at mimicry. He was superbly skilled in the manipulation of his allure. He could draw them in like trout, ready for catch-and-release.

I nudge him again. Dive now, into love. Dive, into crazy love.

But something else entirely happened. In a moment, it was I, me, myself as Hannah-Naomi, who was drawn into crazy love.

I fell in love with Gershom Holder.

Just like that.

Nevermind my guardianship responsibilities to Artemisia. This was the world spinning, swirling, upside-down and backwards, this way and that way, into unknown destinations.

I, Hannah-Naomi, was out of control. In one turbulent downdraft, I was flying, floating, and then, a Fallen Angel.

Chava

1

Well, well. Sounds like a fine mess you got yourself into, Hannah-Naomi. How can a Guardian Angel fall in love? Doesn't that negate your incarnation as a Guardian Angel? Explain to me how this could have happened? And, are you not, at this moment in Angelology, aren't you still required to get permission from the Creation Director? You are doing things the old-fashioned way at this point? Right? You still need to get your guardianship instructions from the Creation Director. You have not yet become a Gig Guardian Angel. Right? What's going on here, Hannah-Naomi?

Hannah-Naomi

1

This was anticipated by the scholars of very distant centuries. The event of a Fallen Angel was predicted. It was written about, this attraction between Guardian Angels and their human counterparts. But look. Look what is known — or thought to be known — about this journey of a soon-to-be Fallen Angel. It is well-recorded in the *Encyclopaedia Judaica:*

> " . . . *A special category of Guardian Angels are the so-called Fallen Angels . . . The earliest report of Fallen Angels is found in the Book of Enoch: The sons of heaven, who belonged to the legion of Guardian Angels, had lusted for the beauty of the daughters of men . . . They consorted with the daughters of men, who gave birth to a generation of giants who set about mercilessly destroying human beings . . . The story of Fallen Angels . . . when they arrived on earth, was that they were seduced by the daughters of men.*"

So goes the story of Fallen Angels — formerly Guardian Angels. But I have to ask: how did those scholars know so much about Fallen Angels?

And note this:

It is clear that the Fallen Angels in this entry from the *Encyclopaedia Judaica* were males. And they fell for and were seduced by the beauty of daughters of men. Clearly, there is no reference to female Guardian Angels experiencing such a thing with the sons of men.

And I ask again: how did the scholars KNOW what they said they knew about Guardian Angels? Especially that part — so graphic the wording — *lusted for*, *seduced by* — how did those learned scholars KNOW about angels falling and being seduced by the daughters of men?

2

However, I must ask this: What about me? What about me, Hannah-Naomi? Could not I — indeed, did not I — become seduced by a son of men? This is very dangerous ground. Oh, and I fell alright. I fell thus hard and was seduced by a particular son of men.

So begins the story of this Fallen Angel, me, Hannah-Naomi.

I turned away from those two artists, one of whom, Artemisia, I had pledged to the Creation Director to be Guardian Angel for her entire lifetime. And the other one, Gershom Holder, I had turned away from even the potential for providing to him guardianship and protection. I turned away for a single moment and then, fell. Fell hard. Crashed into the earth. It was love. Flying, falling, floating. Into the abyss. And as I fell, I would soon enough become one of the Fallen Angels, falling, falling from the esteemed ranks of Guardian Angels. Falling, ill-advised, into love, seduced by the beauty of one of the sons of men — Gershom Holder.

Ah, the irony. I longed for his passion. I lusted for Gershom in his human form and longed for myself to be able to respond in my own human form. I wanted to become a human being, a woman.

I turned away from Artemisia, my artist, my charge, for just a few seconds. For just a few seconds, seeking conjunction with blissful human love, I turned my attention to Gershom. I turned away for a few luxurious seconds to consider, to bathe in, my feelings of desire for love, for this other human being, this man, one of the sons of men.

It was during those moments that my guardianship veered off. An impediment to my duty as Guardian Angel stepped forward and made itself more powerful, overwhelming me. I longed to become a human woman.

It is believed and debated, and there is hubristic certainty — a tone and manner to these teachings that demonstrates a cocky attitude — Yes, the scholars sound so cock-sure when they write it down that:

On some extraordinary occasions Guardian Angels may assume the shape of human beings.

CHAVA

1

BUT HANNAH-NAOMI. Isn't that impossible? I don't understand. Here I am arguing. With a Guardian Angel, no less. Gig Guardian Angel. Right here in my studio. Sitting on my sofa. How can this be? I ask again. I have sometimes quipped that I am a card-carrying member in the Diaspora of the Discombobulated. But really! This one is over the top!

You, dear reader, might just as well throw this book across the room. You do not need my craziness, not in crazy times like these, here in 2022. I can't blame you though. This announcement that a Guardian Angel falls in love with a mortal man leaves me gasping. It's unreal. So is Hannah-Naomi real? Is she unreal?

I am so confused.

Hannah-Naomi

1

Well, if you just pay attention, Chava, things will shake down and you'll at least get the gist of my story. Listen up and learn! But, in essence, you are correct. And along with this coincidence, I received a vivid insight into Gershom that would influence him for the rest of his life. My perspective on him broadened. All of this in a clarion flash of intuition.

But along with this insight came a flood of other contextual information.

As a Guardian Angel, I had been blessed with several tricks of the guardianship trade. One of these was an ability to see into the future of some human souls. The pros and cons of a long future life for Gershom Holder flooded my mind. Not only could I preview major events of his life but I could also see and assess the influence of time and place upon this human man as well. And so, context came with foreknowledge. The whole history of the future plopped into my consciousness at that very moment that I lost guardianship abilities and fell in love with Gershom. However, sadly, this would be the last bit of foreknowledge that I was to experience as I left my Guardian Angelic self and exchanged it for the love of a human woman. I would not experience this kind of illuminated vision until later, much later, when I was allowed to resume being a Guardian Angel. But I'm jumping ahead of myself. Patience, Chava. I will get there.

Chava

1

Tell me more, Hannah-Naomi. I want to hear more about how you fell in love with Gershom.

Hannah-Naomi

1

And the weather changed and it was springtime, senior year of college for Gershom, and little cupids, stupid cupids, flitting about chubby and cherubic with their tiny flightless wings and all of that and they aimed their arrows and those pinprick, stupid arrows, stupid, and they aimed poorly, missing my Gershom and hitting their mark on me instead — and it was time for love.

Not for Gershom. For me.

Suddenly it hit me, one of those pesky pinpricking arrows. I snatched it out of my arm and threw it violently onto the ground. But too late. I was already overwhelmed by a crazy stupid zeal for human love; thanks to the ministrations of those stupid cherubs.

Now I lusted after a Very Great Love. Of my own. With the ease of my nascent cupidity — a trait that would some day blossom in me as a further result of my falling in love with Gershom — I turned away from my guardianship duties, hungry for mortality, thirsting to drink it in: LUV. I had lost my conscience entirely. I floundered. But, most important: I turned away from my focus on Artemisia, turned away — idiot! Selfish Fallen Angel — I lost my focus and went mad with needing love. I fell in love with this man, this Gershom, with his beauty and even with his indifference, which deftly drew me in. Instead of remaining devoted to Artemisia, as her Guardian Angel, I fell in love with him, Gershom Holder, in all his splendor, with him as he was: a mortal man. Not perfect. As is. But good enough.

I failed. I failed. After flying, floating, I fell. I fell in love with a mortal man. I was done for. And with my newfound human foibles, I began to craft my excuses: oh well, the heart has its reasons. But it would play out poorly, as I would discover later. Meanwhile, I, a Guardian Angel, was fallen, in love, with a mortal man.

More the fool, I.

It was time to talk with the Creation Director.

2

I pleaded with the Creation Director:

"Please. Please. Please allow me to assume the shape of a human woman. I am begging you. Please."

The Creation Director responds to my pleading:

"And why should I do this thing, Hannah-Naomi? You realize, Hannah-Naomi, what you seek is well-nigh to profane. It is even, I might add, a desecration of your responsibilities of guardianship. By desiring to become a human being, you have already left behind many of your traditional guardianship duties that you pledged to Artemisia at her birth. And get over any notion that you can be both — both a Guardian Angel AND a human woman. Why don't you simply transform yourself, dear Hannah-Naomi, into the human woman you desire to be? Isn't that possible, Hannah-Naomi? You claim you have, and can assert, Freewill. Well then, do it.

"Instead, you now ask me for permission to be transformed into a human woman? To enter the ranks of the mortal? Which, you do realize, includes the iron-clad law that each and every single human mortal shall die. This is perverse. You want the near-impossible. To live as a human woman, yet you must take it all or nothing. To be human, you may be able to experience love and human passion, but you must also die. And now you beg me for it? Now you beg? You have such gall, Hannah-Naomi. You, who even declared that Guardian Angels could act without getting permission from the Creation Director. Now you ask me? You beg me? Ironic this is, Hannah-Naomi."

I resume my pleading:

"I cannot explain. I know this however: this feeling is real. This feeling has provided me with a taste of what human love can be. Its passions. Its compulsions. I cannot explain it in full because I have not yet experienced it in its wholeness. But I do know this: the heart has its reasons for which reason knows nothing of."

The Creation Director opens a fresh pack of Camels, shakes a few forward, and gestures it toward me. I pick one out, thumb and first finger pinching it up and out of the pack, graceful, a sweet feminine gesture to beguile my Creation Director, and I lodge it, businesslike, into the corner of my mouth. We are at an impasse.

"You are, Hannah-Naomi, near to blasphemous. Most certainly, you are being highly irresponsible. I see by your beseeching that you are close already to being human. Irrational. Self absorbed. Your behavior, with this outrageous request places you among the secular — not caring for morals, ethics, or justice, justice. The iniquity of your request places you almost among the sinful. You want that for your legacy? You seek this thing, this transformation into a human woman? That's it?"

"Yes. Please. More than anything."

"And for what? For this handsome, fallible human man with his cigarettes?"

The Creation Director mocks my request. I know this. Trying to change my mind, my very heart.

"He handles his Camels so masterfully? For that!? You beg me for human attributes. How noble. How strong. You, Hannah-Naomi, are gullible and foolish. You have been seduced by a son of men. And you yearn for human connection with this man? And let's not be coy, you yearn for sex with him? This is very dangerous ground. This is not love. This is a seduction. You are nothing to this son of men. You are foolish to believe that you are otherwise in the psyche of this son of men. Hannah-Naomi, this too will pass. But do not delude yourself that this love, so-called, will bring you anything but harm. You are about to turn your world upside-down."

The Creation Director is fuming, then says to me:

"Not to mention, you will turn the world of your charge, Artemisia Gershom, with whom you have been tasked with a lifetime of guardianship. You will most certainly turn upside-down her world as well. You would even have warned Artemisia about the danger of such a seduction as you now are begging for. You would urge or nudge or otherwise warn her against this kind of relationship. Yet in your own case, you are blinded."

For now, I could not hear that warning. I responded with:

"I am willing to try. I am needful of this. I need to experience my own human love with, as you put it, this particular son of men."

3

And, just like that, I became Gershom's girlfriend. Neither girl nor friend, nor guardian, nor *what* exactly? A hybrid I became. Maybe, inflamed with my presence as a human woman, as a potential girlfriend, maybe Gershom would someday call me *angel*. If he called me his angel, in that case, would that make me one?

Chava

1

Somehow what I found in Hannah-Naomi, here as a visitor in my studio, what I discovered, as her story progressed, was that she was trying to rationalize herself to me. What for? Did she need to confess and to make excuses to me, a human being, a woman? And, what was I to do? Was I to bless and forgive her for her indiscretions, for her mistakes? Did she believe that, by somehow unburdening herself and her complicated story onto me, that all would be forgiven?

What was going on here?

Did she select me as her confessor because I could write? Or did she think that because I was also an artist, that I would one day illustrate her complicated confession? Did she believe that by telling me all of this, her past history, that I would make a report about her behavior into a public creation, a book, for example, or a massive mural on the dome of a vast building?

This was getting weird. I was starting to feel awkward. And, worse, I was beginning to distrust Hannah-Naomi. I started to feel like she intended to use me for her own ulterior motives. I had this sinking sensation that she needed me to make excuses for and, worse, to require me to ameliorate her past behaviors. And I did not like this. Not one bit. Now, I sat back in my chair, tipping backwards, and I began to view her with skepticism. With doubt. This was not pleasant. This changed our relationship and I did not want to go any further.

Hannah-Naomi

1

Inspired by my human female passions, like some blithering lovelorn poet, I gathered about me a threadbare rationale: I could become a human woman and still be a Guardian Angel. Simultaneously, I could continue my guardianship duties to Artemisia and even add Gershom for other guardianship duties. I could be both to both of them. I was, after all, a Guardian Angel who could multi-task.

You may ask, 'isn't that impossible?' and, yes, of course it would have been.

It was completely deranged. Idiotic. What I wanted to do was impossible. But says who? Why believe any of the rules and regulations and concepts of how Guardian Angels should or do behave when nobody, not a single human soul, even the wisest scholar, can attest to having met or spoken to a genuine Guardian Angel? Isn't it time to do things differently? Don't I exercise Freewill ? Can't I use my own Freewill to make my own decisions, to act in my own unique way? Who says I can't? Therefore, I will be Guardian Angel for two human souls. AND I shall embody myself as both: Guardian Angel and as the girlfriend, ever-human and simultaneously passionate, as a woman?

That's possible.

Isn't it?

Isn't it?

And with these muddled thoughts, these ideas of using my own Freewill, willy-nilly, I finagled in my wandering heart, a new way to be a Guardian Angel and to be an embodied human woman as well. Some angels may become human beings? Right? Some human beings may become angels. How about both? Well, now I wanted to do this thing. To be both. I have Freewill. I can do this.

As Pascal said, and with this being me, at this crossroads:

"The heart has its reasons, for which reason knows nothing of."

As I said: just like that, I was in love with Gershom Holder. Instantly. Irretrievably.

Chava

1

Hannah-Naomi sounds more and more irrational. Less and less angelic. She babbles. She makes wobbly assertions to substantiate, to rationalize, her intended behaviors — her desire to be both a Guardian Angel and a human woman. This is disturbing to me. This is almost worse than my delusional belief that there is, actually, a real Guardian Angel right here in my studio.

Hannah-Naomi

1

Remember that list of Guardian Angelic attributes, Chava? The one that claimed that Guardian Angels can foretell the future? Well, during my eons of tenure as a Guardian Angel I have been able to see into or to intuit events in the futures of many of my charges. Yet, as I reflect back upon some of these sightings, I have difficulty expressing how, exactly, these visions or intuitions presented themselves to me.

In some instances, a view into the future presented in the manner that you human beings call *a still small voice*. In these cases, I would just experience an ineffable thump of my heart or a trembling of my wings. It would be enough for me to nudge my charge into some inward attention to their own memory work.

Then there were other instances of future foretelling during which I was presented with a collage of images.

Snapshots, flipping and spinning, each one a picture of something that would appear to one or another of my charges, visual elements that would one day require that person to act, to do, to complete, or even to escape from a future event.

Then there were other forms of foretelling futures — sometimes a friend or a relative of one of my charges would blurt something out and I could perceive that those words were going to influence my charge some time in the future — to influence that charge to DO something that may have been unperceived by that particular charge, but to whom the words of that friend or relative would be of very great influence upon them in the future.

Then there was this experience:

In a weird coincidence, this particular vision of the future crashed in upon my consciousness at the exact moment that I fell in love with Gershom Holder. The future that it foretold was for both of our futures — my future and the future of Gershom.

The first item I experienced was my own beating heart, a fluttering heart, but not a fluttering of wings. I embodied winglessness. I embodied giggling. I embodied embarrassment. A pain in the belly. I embodied myself as a young human woman, wordlessly loving, or believing that she loved, a human man, namely Gershom Holder. Then it was gone. I was no longer a Guardian Angel. I no longer had anything in me that could foresee the future. I was a silly, senseless, ridiculous human girl. I could no longer foretell the future. But I was now embodied in the future.

The second thing I experienced, simultaneously and viscerally with my first moment of falling in love with Gershom, was a kind of gut-wrenching terror, an intense feeling of guilt, then of hatred, then of silent grieving. These feelings inside me were all rolled up into one shaking crash. And all of these feelings were to me simultaneous with my feelings of having been transformed into an embodied young woman.

Yet, alongside the coincidences of these two separate flashing visions into my future and into Gershom's future, I knew that these visions of the future would influence Gershom Holder, and would influence me as well, for the rest of our lives.

In just a few days before Gershom's college graduation ceremonies, he would experience wrenching terror along with intense guilt and hatred and then of silent grieving. These feelings inside me were all rolled up into one shaking crash.

Listen up, Chava. This is important.

2

This is the story of a near-miss in a Cessna. What happened to that little aircraft on a clear and lovely spring afternoon high above the California desert? It will take forty-five years for Gershom Holder, to navigate the dangers of that flight. Listen, Chava:

The dorm echoes with the sounds of finals week. Up

and down the halls — guffaws, doors slamming, scuffing boots, coffee cups clanking. Chanting is heard: algebraic equations, lists of flora and fauna, mumblings, shouts of despair. The phone rings.

"It's for you, Gershom."

On the other end he hears the measured tones of The Pilot:

"Where are you, Ger? Are you okay?"

It is that tone of voice every son knows and that every son's parent uses when something is wrong, just plain wrong. The question is slowly intoned, each word clipped. Where the heck does he think I am?

"I'm fine Dad. I'm in my dorm room. I'm. I'm. I'm studying for art history. The final is tomorrow."

"Are you okay?" The Pilot reasserts himself. Not unusual when he wants to make a point.

"Yes, I'm fine. Fine. What? What is it?"

Nothing. The Pilot continues in a calmer tone, anodyne comments about turbulent weather on the way home from a short hop up over the desert.

"Well, Ger. Best of luck tomorrow — on your, ah — civics test."

Then with urgency Gershom cuts in: "But, what's wrong, Dad? What is it? What's up?"

"Nothing, Gershom."

"But, Dad!"

"Get a grip, Ger."

The Pilot signs off. Click.

What was that?

3

Graduation ceremony is successfully achieved. All of Gershom's finals are, if not stellar, certainly adequate. After the hooding ceremony, with his cowls flapping, sliding, unaccustomed and foreign around his narrow shoulders, a friend of Gershom's in line, clutching his own diploma, turns around and asks:

"What are we going to do now, Gershom?"

A few months later, casually, apropos of nothing in the previous conversation that would bring up the subject of the near-miss in the Cessna, The Pilot mumbles, as if to himself:

"There was some heavy turbulence on the way home last month over the desert."

Nothing more. Subject closed. There were always more important things to worry about than a little turbulence in the Cessna.

Once or twice, several years later, and at peculiar intervals in the mystery, there were mentions, casual, in passing, mumbled: The Pilot had had to put the Cessna into a spin in order to save it. It had been caught in an updraft, rapidly, uncontrollably, pushed into an elevation to where he would not have been able to breathe. The Cessna had no oxygen capabilities or equipment. The Pilot forced the plane way down in elevation by putting it into a spin. Gershom thought he had heard it as *a tail spin*. But he was never quite sure about that. The Pilot informed him that the weather condition that created those sudden swift updrafts was generally indicated by lenticular cloud formations that a pilot could see before takeoff, very high up in the sky. There had not been any lenticular cloud formations upon takeoff. After the near-miss, The Pilot steered the small craft home, just like that, really low and really slow. Nothing more was said about the incident. No details. Certainly, no dramatics. The Pilot steered away completely from the subject. The end.

4

The next thing Gershom hears about that flight will be in forty years. The Pilot, by then, is struggling up and down among his mind's choppy altitudes — maneuvering from one episode to another, one era after another, up and down, up and down, off course, herky-jerky. Then, out of nowhere one day, he says to Gershom:

"Remember that flight home over the desert?"

"Yeah, what happened?"

"We opened the cockpit doors."

Then The Pilot was gone, hard to port and off again, into the murky visibility of Alzheimer's, destination unknown, impassable for Gershom. The Pilot would not, or could not, speak further about that particular flight, the near-miss of the Cessna. But in his head he heard, over the shriek of the Cessna's motor, the words of a Royal Air Force instructor:

"Fly by the seat of yer pants, Chiefy. Belt your butt, clot. Quit yer binding. How 'bout a little scream downhill for this junkheap, eh matey? Will that work for now? Go ahead, Chiefy. Show us how it's done. Live up to your name, Holder. Get a grip."

Years later, with the serendipity of Facebook, a former colleague of Gershom's popped up. Dave. From back in his corporate days. Emailing back and forth, updating their lives for the past several dozen years, Dave mentioned to Gershom that he had obtained his private pilot's license and had owned a Cessna for several years.

"Us too," said Gershom. "We flew all over the place when I was a kid."

Gershom told Dave about the near miss in their Cessna. Then he asked Dave about the weather conditions over the desert and if he knew anything about those harbingers of pending danger for Cessna pilots: lenticular cloud formations. Dave did indeed know. He had had some experiences with dangerous updrafts. He, Dave, had felt it was sheer luck that he had made it back alive one time. Dave supposed that The Pilot had had special training during his Royal Air Force service. Dave knew that The Pilot had flown in the Royal Air Force for six years during World War II. So Dave figured that The Pilot had had advanced pilot training to survive extreme dangers of all kinds while in flight.

Then Gershom asked Dave what he thought The Pilot had meant when he said:

"We opened the cockpit doors."

Dave responded instantly:

"He thought they were going down."

"How do you know that, Dave?"

"When a pilot of a small craft realizes that it will crash, he opens the cockpit doors so that, if they do crash, and the craft rolls onto the ground, there will be a way out. The Pilot had thought that the Cessna was going down."

Gershom remembers when The Pilot said:

"Remember that flight home over the desert?"

"Yeah, what happened, Dad?"

"We opened the cockpit doors."

"You never said that before, Dad. How come? How come you never told me what happened up there? How come you never told me that? I was about to graduate from college. Didn't you ever think how that would be for me? An orphan at my own graduation? And you don't think I, in a sense, somehow deserved to hear what happened that day? Was entitled to hear? I'm your son. It's not like I couldn't take a shock or something. Is it? Is it? After all we'd been through already? Me, after all I had been through — with my Bar Mitzva and all that. How come you never told me about the near-miss in our Cessna? Tell me. Tell me, Dad. Maybe it was a Guardian Angel? Ya think? Maybe?"

"Don't talk nonsense, Gershom."

"You are being needlessly secretive. Evasive. Why, Dad?"

"Always with your lip, Gershom."

"You owe me, Dad. You and your silence, your British

machismo. It's hurtful. It's brutal. Do you know? Do you? Can't you see what I mean? You . . . you are . . ."

"Get a grip, Ger."

As usual: Gershom is shut down.

There he goes again. Off into the wild blue yonder. How useful, that cliché. But this time, The Pilot is keeping the cockpit doors shut tight, latched. No talking to Gershom. Not even a boastful reminiscence. Not a word for Gershom. Going down again? Looks like it. Words fail.

5

Now, here's another slant on how that near-miss was avoided.

The Cessna may have been saved by extraordinary aeronautic skills gained by The Pilot during his service in the Royal Air Force. If this pilot had been involved in a secretive and advanced Royal Air Force pilot training program, The Pilot may have had, in his bag of tricks, extraordinary aeronautical techniques for saving the Cessna that day.

If.

There was, in the several years before the United States entered World War II, a secret program to provide special training to pilots in the Royal Air Force. The program was dubbed: The Towers Scheme. It was named after U.S. Admiral Towers. It was a way to enhance RAF pilot training and took place with Royal Air Force pilots who trained at several U.S. bases in various states in the

United States. The Towers Scheme began around 1941 — before the United States entered that world war. It was arranged, by back channels, between Prime Minister Winston Churchill and President Franklin Delano Roosevelt. It lasted for several years, continuing into the United States' involvement in World War II.

Particular to The Pilot, he was part of the Towers Scheme and trained at the U.S. Naval Air force station in Pensacola, Florida. Advanced training was completed at Pensacola and there were 2,775 pilots who graduated. They were all awarded both U.S. Navy Air Corps and Royal Air Force wings for their uniforms. The Towers Scheme provided advanced training for Coastal Command. It included training for Observers, Wireless Operators, Air-Gunners, as well as Pilots. One of the cadets from the program commented in his own recent online memoire:

> ***"The hard-earned Solid Silver Wings of the U.S. Navy Air Corps that we proudly wore on the right breast of our tunics along with our Royal Air Force Wings which the U.S. had thoughtfully pre-ordered, on the left. Later back in the UK, we were forbidden to wear the U.S. Silver Wings, an order which most of us ignored."***

—

As did, apparently, The Pilot of the Cessna of the near-miss. In the photographs of their wedding, on the left of The Pilot's tunic there resided the Royal Air Force Wings and on the right side there were the Solid Silver Wings of the U. S. Navy Air Corps.

Proof, perhaps, that not every near-miss was averted because of the intersession of a Guardian Angel.

Now, four decades later, The Pilot, hears that strident voice, the shouts of his training officer, bellowing into his headphones over the deafening PBY engine and props:

"Listen up, troop. Always fly by the seat of yer pants. Are you listening? Fly, always, and do not forget: Fly by the seat of yer pants, Holder, and get a grip, gentlemens."

CHAVA

1

WELL, YES. I CAN SEE how earth-bound events could have superseded the workings of a Guardian Angel.

But did you, Hannah-Naomi, lend a nudge to The Pilot? Did you remind him of the memory of his RAF flight instructor shouting at him to fly by the seat of his pants? Was the near miss with the Cessna a bit of memory work spanning decades — bits and pieces of how The Pilot saved the Cessna from the killing updraft? And then, Hannah-Naomi, were the clues that came to Gershom Holder also nudges from you? First he learns that The Pilot opened the cockpit doors; then, later, Gershom learns that The Pilot thought the craft was going down; then, even later, Gershom learns about the secret flight training program, the Towers Scheme, and how it may have helped to save The Pilot. And you infer that these were flashes of insight that you could later use in memory work with Gershom when you returned to being a Guardian Angel?

I must say, Hannah-Naomi, you thicken the plot in your story. You lead me, your audience, down a rabbit hole. This is not easy to keep track of. Oh, well. If you are but a hallucination of mine, I suppose all of these complications are of my own making and stem from somewhere deep within my own subconscious.

Right?

Hannah-Naomi

1

But to return to Artemisia and Gershom:

Both of my charges, Gershom Holder and Artemisia Gershom, had fathers who had been pilots in that mid-century war. And, as if that were not enough coincidence, both of their mother's died before Gershom and Artemisia were fully adults. Sad. Odd that, yes? They were both strangers in the strange land of the dead-end road of mortality in human affairs. They both became strangers in that strange land of those who witness, before full adulthood, parents who disappear into the World to Come. They both grew into their given names: Gershoms both of them: *strangers in that land*.

2

On his wedding day, prior to the end of the Second

World War, The Pilot wore his dress uniform with its two sets of wings. With those wings on display, it begs the question: why not believe in further assistance, throughout a lifetime, from the wings of a Guardian Angel?

3

The bride and groom pose for photographs in their starched and pressed uniforms just minutes after their vows. They stand there, grinning like fools in love have always done when facing the bridal photographer with his intrusive camera.

The Pilot, now husband, stands, ramrod, fists balled along the sides of his pressed pantlegs. The camera captures his two sets of pilots' wings, one on each side of his Royal Air Force Service Dress uniform. She, now a wife, stands slender and chic in her Mainbocher U.S. Navy Dress Blue Uniform. She is a U.S. Navy Gunnery Instructor. Her Dress Uniform, a six-gore skirt, grazes her knees showing off the best of the wartime shortages.

The bride and groom had just turned twenty-two. Teenagers, almost. Still. What a time to make a lifetime commitment, a war still raging. What common sense it was to get married then, yes? Well, it was so romantic. So dangerous: danger, the fuel to heat up urgent youthful romance. He will be shipped out in two days. The newlyweds did not know when, or if, he would ever return. At least they had this: their ceremony, short and tender, consecrated in a tiny New York chapel that specialized in the wartime service of providing scarce and hastily produced military weddings. No waiting.

That was love, Gershom. Those were your parents.

4

Remember when I said the two charges I have been working with have something in common? Oh, not just their names: Gershom Holder and Artemisia Gershom. There's more: both of my charges — first Artemisia Gershom whom I joined at her birth, then later, Gershom Holder who I met when Artemisia was in college — both of these human souls, to whom I would eventually become Guardian Angel, had had fathers in the military. Both of their fathers had been pilots too, during that airborne war which flew around the globe at that time in history.

How strange, such simultaneous coincidences. As their stories were revealed to me over time, I discovered striking parallels in their lives.

5

In the case of Gershom Holder, by the time The Pilot, his father, got to the San Fernando Valley, Gershom was a willful toddler. When his grandmother handed him, squirming, into his father's arms, The Pilot was, if not shell-shocked, certainly numbed and slightly crazy from the war. He took hold of Gershom awkwardly, reluctantly, and Gershom shrieked, squirmed, and shat.

Then he handed Gershom back. His Grandmother never forgave that gesture. She never gave The Pilot an inch of her good will. Pretty soon, she kicked all three out of her household.

The Pilot, your mother, and you, Gershom, were tossed from home and hearth and safety.

Poor child-mother and child-Pilot and their baby-child: a suit of clothing, a dusty RAF trunk, an entrenching tool, alone in orange-grove, dirt-road Reseda, with their baby, demanding and wiggly. The world war's new parents, Gershom's parents, were alone in the night in the post-war-prosperity of this strange land. All they had, these kids and their kid, was their military uniforms and arm patches, citizen soldiers now, both of them, of the Good War, refugees too, rewarded with that universal badge of courage — an outrageous mother-in-law.

My point? There was another form of mental stress and potentially deep psychological damage done to some World War II vets who returned, physically undamaged, but emotionally wounded and sadly distant from babies with whom they had never bonded. And never would.

As I learned more about Gershom Holder and his father and his mother, I saw that Artemisia, too, would be subjected to a certain kind of post-war parental dynamic. Artemisia, too, was a child of a soldier-pilot in that war.

—

6

The romance of both sets of parents created an urgency in the mothers, in particular, to have a baby, a souvenir, in case their respective husbands never came home from that war. Having these babies while the fathers were away in the theatres of conflict would give birth to another war-related marital stress that did not quite turn out the way the women may have hoped. Artemisia's mother was loyal to a fault to her pilot-husband. 'Til death. Gershom's mother showed all good faith that their little family would be bonded by the adventures and romance of flying in their little Cessna.

There were to be unintended consequences, however. I have named it Secondary Familial PTSD. I observed it in both Gershom and Artemisia as I learned more about each of them.

Many of the friends of both Artemisia and Gershom had the same framed pictures on top of their brand-new TVs: their parents' weddings, the men in uniform.

Some effects of Secondary Familial PTSD may still be experienced today in the now-adult children of soldiers from that generation. It consists of a blindness in the hearts of the returning soldiers. For them, a fog billows around, decreasing visibility of the infant offspring of these men, these virtual teenage men, who survived their country's conflicts only to return home to new and other unexpected conflicting expectations of their new civilian lives. Make a decent living. Provide for children you do not even know. And where is that beautiful passionate woman I married? At times these men may have wondered if it would not have been better to have been shot down instead. That fate would have, at least, left them heroes. Do not think about that now. If ever.

What kind of parents were they? Former teenagers who were formed by world conflicts way too urgent and complex for their meager middlebrow upbringings back then. After all, the generation of the parents of those young men were Victorians. By the time of the 20th Century, Victorian thinking was like vapor floating up into the ceilings. The parents of Gershom and Artemisia urged a bankrupt form of patriotism on them. Join the forces. Do your bit. Help keep American housing tracts occupied and well-mortgaged, of course, when you come home from that war. Act like all the others, like themselves, who have their wedding photographs on top of their brand-new TVs. A neighbor, a Navy man, for example, with his bride wearing a short green suit with a flower pinned onto her lapel — those two, same as your parents, teenagers or just about, the brides so excited to be pregnant.

"I will have a child to remember him by, just in case he does not return to me from the war."

And finally they are all back home, baby and all, and the Fifties and the Sixties fly by, the glass of bourbon, glass of Gallo, mint julip, Scotchrocks, Manhattans are always ready to hand on the little end tables that perch next to brand new davenports. Television started invading living rooms and influenced thinking. TV brought mundane wifely wit to those mothers: Lucy, Ozzie and Harriet, and fathers Knowing Best — all those messages of that time. Too loud, too often, the TVs, and nobody ever again looks or gives a thought to what it really meant. Nobody sees, really sees, the wedding photos on top of the TVs and the "short skirts we wore back then and the notions we had." Oh, my.

Scotch, bourbon, gin — from jelly glasses at first, then later, in new fancy cut-glass stemware — goblets always half empty, half-full.

Aren't we happy now?
Weren't we happy, back then?
And then?
And then?
We had a nice life.
Didn't we?
We sacrificed everything for you.
Every.
Single.
Thing.

7

But perhaps I am talking too much. These are things and feelings and events and attitudes, held in memories, and they could be useful in your development as a full and adult human being, as artists, even. But perhaps it is too soon for you to grasp these ideas. To *get,* through the retranscription of memories, how they made you who you are, Artemisia and Gershom. Later. If ever. Artemisia Gershom may sink into unconsciousness. Gershom Holder may sink into silence with:

"Get a grip, Ger."

Chava

1

Well, of course, Hannah-Naomi, we are all jumbled up with our inherited skillsets, talents, IQs, and miscellaneous DNA that goes back into each of our own dimly lit family histories. Then, too, on top of innate qualities, we human beings are surrounded by the people and places that we occupy in time and by the moments in world histories that we will both witness and participate in. Put it all together and what kind of life, what kind of person, will be the result? It will be a hodge-podge for certain.

If every single human being among the billions who inhabit this small blue dot of a planet, floating as it does in the dark universe of other billions of dots — well, what I am floundering around to say is this: it's no wonder there is so much discombobulation inside each of us human souls. Sheesh. How is it even remotely possible that this onslaught of internal and of external influences, on each of us as human beings, how is it remotely possible that things will just turn out to be okay and merely okay?

2

And now, you, Hannah-Naomi, have arrived in my studio. Now you, Hannah-Naomi, are speaking to me, narrating your life as a Guardian Angel. Narrating, as well, the lives of just two of your charges, to whom you have been tasked with Guardian Angelic duties. It's a lot for me to take in. And, worst of all, your being here with me now — well, the implication is that I am bonkers. That I am stark raving mad with hallucinations. It's getting more evident that you, Hannah-Naomi, are a figment of my over-worked imagination. Should I trust you? Should I trust myself?

Listen: There is a Guardian Angel in my studio.

Do you believe in Guardian Angels?

Or not?

I rest my case: I must have gone over the edge. I may not be trusted further.

How about you?

Do you believe me?

Or Hannah-Naomi?

Both?

Neither?

You decide.

Hannah-Naomi

1

Wait, Chava. There's more.

So begins the story of this Fallen Angel, me, Hannah-Naomi. I must continue. Please. You must let me explain. Please understand me. Cast your reason aside. Judge me with your own heart.

In a flash, it happened. No transition. Suddenly, I am just sitting. My elbows rest on a sticky coffeeshop table. I breathe in steam from a hot black liquid in a chipped ceramic cup. I take a tentative sip. Bitter. Hot. Too hot to sip more. Coffee, I do believe. I have seen it before but never tasted it.

Silent, my Very Great Love, Gershom, sits across the table from me. He is there. I am here. Instead of Gershom Holder, a potential boyfriend for Artemisia whom I had been tasked to Guardianship, it was Gershom Holder with me. I was sitting here, having coffee, with him, my Very Great Love.

He grasps with both hands the sides of his mug of coffee, cigarette burning between his knuckles, smoke wafting, suggestive, mute. He says nothing. This is Brontë stuff. Romance Novel Stuff. Chick-Lit themes: silent brooding male with hysterical female stuck back home wasting away in some attic. Classic stuff of human female lore and literature. The women suffering, suffering, never knowing the extent to which it is because of the man in her life that is the source of all that ennui. I know about these things: I was, formerly, a Guardian Angel to some females and now I am a female human being myself.

I study the profile of my man, my Very Great Love, and respond only to the peculiar sensations of having — without previous warning — having suddenly become a human woman. Slight pain in the lower belly. Band across my ribcage. A bra? I tug a strap that slides down my upper arm, squirm it back in place. It's too tight. I am so hot. Is this what it is to be a human woman who is in love with a human man? A daughter of men in passionate contemplation of a son of men?

In addition, I observe a new feeling in myself: a sense of justification, righteousness, prevarication. I stifle a giggle. I'm a girl. With my new intellect careening around my flitting mind, I start to rationalize: Artemisia does not need a Guardian Angel. Probably Gershom does not require one either. Neither of them require someone to constantly nag about doing this thing or that thing. They are both fully capable on their own. She's about to graduate from college now. She's a grown-up now. I rationalize. I tell myself lies, proud of my human female skills at twisting the truth. I am in love after all. Sitting here with my Very Great Love, I make excuses — Gershom is fully capable on his own. After all. I have not been his Guardian Angel since he was born. Look at him. Just look. Yes, look. He can do without a Guardian Angel. What he needs is a — what? — a GIRLFRIEND.

I swoon.

Excuses, excuses. I sink and thrash in sophistry as I experience this new human feeling, how it feels to lie about my motives — well not lie, exactly, but let's call it obfuscation, and to lie, in another sense of *to lie*, to lie with another human creature. Heavenly. And, oh well, so what? To abandon my responsibilities. My former instinct to protect and to guide Artemisia fades into self-destructive human indifference, wild rationalization, and, instead, I lurch into human passion, powerful longing. Oh well. So be it. I am in love. Flying, falling, floating. I shall live my own life. My life. My feelings. My own Very Great Love. I shall live my life however I damn-well choose. I can't remember which wise scholar ever concluded that: Angels have no evil intentions. I have none. I have only the most compelling, the most intense of intentions — to lie with this human man.

Here is where I belong now — to Gershom Holder.

Golda

1

My name is Golda. My bloodline is that of Golden Labrador Retriever. I am born of a long and proud line of sniffers and fetchers. We are an honorable breed. Steadfast. Useful, even, in our tasks. Our noses are long and sensitive. Skillfully, and with ease, we retrieve things for our human companions. Thus, I prefer being called a Labradorian. More noble of sound, don't you agree? Better for branding. You may call me Goldie. I was chosen to live with this man, an ar-dist, and we live here together in this enormous room. He paints. I pant. I am ever so grateful to, and forever loyal to, this man who saved me from uncertainty, or worse, from misery, from darkness. He said it was my eyes, my beautiful golden brown eyes that caught him. He has tried to paint my eyes any number of times. Without success. I say, who can paint the gaze of a dog, the canine holding fast and deep into a staring and confused human being, unflinching, soul plunging, the fixed attention, the stare of my deep brown eyes that glint from time to time with a sudden spark of refraction, golden. Like my name. Who could paint that? Who would have the temerity to paint my enigmatic canine eyes? Only this man, this ar-dist, so-called, here in this large room, messy enough to entertain my canine heart and he, my ar-dist, tosses a rich and chewy tennis ball halfway across the open dripping paint cans, the torn canvases, brushes propped up in water pitchers. Splashes of paint, as random as Jackson Pollock drops, decorate our floorboards of this one-time warehouse. You think I know nothing of Jackson Pollock? Do not underestimate my vision.

We have a rumpled mattress in the corner. I sniff the coffee cups, half drained, that perch on the edges of an impossible worktable that is piled and scattered with inspiration. And with failures. Let's be honest. I love this room. I love this man. An ar-dist, this man, my god, the one who embraced me to his chest, me a puppy, unformed, doomed, and brought me here to our home, clutching me to his chest inside his jacket, and named me Goldie right then and there, golden warm, and made me wonder when he asked me:

"Where did you come from my Golden Girl?"

—

2

And we loved one another, barely speaking, because if we said too much our luck could turn on us and we would be lost to one another and he taught me:

"Never say the word 'luck'.' If you accidentally say this word, Goldie, quickly knock wood three times. You can use your tail, or, lacking wood, bump your paw against your head three times to dispel the evil inclinations of the yetzer ha-ra. Never tempt it, Goldie. Ever. Stay golden my little one. Tu, tu, tu."

And my ar-dist painted dogs — never in my own image. He painted dogs in honest response to my fidelity. And thus we lived.

3

We have a cat here in the studio. Did I mention that? She says almost nothing, yet she sits in feline judgment, assessing me quite stringently. She disdains what she considers to be my sniveling canine admiration for our ar-dist. This is not upsetting to me, but it would be more companionable if she and I could simply just sit around and chat.

Cat. Chat. Ha! Fat chance that. Fat!

The cat speaks another language. Not my tongue. But words of her own in her own tongue I suppose. Yawning, licking her lips, she rises, bows in downward facing dog — a yoga pose that I can do much better.

It is said in the commentaries found in the Aggadah of biblical and post-biblical times that on special occasions angels may assume the shape of men or of animals. You question my knowledge of the commentaries? Do not doubt my background. Having not the language tools that reside in the human palate and in its larynx, we canines must, of needs, keep our ascension to Guardian Angel status to ourselves. It is, however, common among human beings to believe in their hearts that we household canines are, indeed, their guardians, and most certainly, that we are their Guardian Angels. That is my story.

That may also be the story of the cat we live with in this ar-dist's studio. Although she must speak for herself on this topic and I already know that she is very tight-lipped when it comes to her beliefs, her origins, her heart's desires.

Oh well. This is my story and I will tell it any-which-way I please.

4

Then one day my ar-dist stepped into our studio with a new girlfriend. I sensed along my spine such a tremor, such a glint of cosmic illumination, such a fright that my fur stood on end from forehead to tail, stood on end, and I shook violently and spun around, three times clockwise and three times counter clockwise, to try to dispel my embodiment of anxiety. This deeply alarmed my ar-dist and he rushed to grab my spinning body. Drawing me near enough to almost crush me, he held me firm and I could hear his beating heart and feel his temperature rise. He held me so fast that I could perceive other changes within his chest, surges of violent irreconcilable fear as he may have felt that I would die thus, shaking and trembling, in his arms.

Something was changed.

Some thing had entered our world.

That thing was the new girlfriend.

As I settled down a bit and with only my extended flapping and dripping tongue attesting to my remaining fears, I approached the girl, wafting sideways back and forth to get a better sniff of this being, to see if she were both a girl and a friend, for I received absolutely not one reference from her posture, from her body, not a single hint that she contained girl-ness nor friend-ship.

In my pervasive fear and misery, I quickly discerned that she was in heat. Yes. She did smell of blood. She herself confirmed this to me by surreptitiously reaching behind her rump to search for the stickiness of her own blood on her clothing. I felt for her, I really did as a fellow female, although that feeling did not diffuse my anxiety. It simply was that this simulacrum of a human being was in heat and it was as if she did not know what she should do. Already she was being propelled by lust for the ar-dist, yet she seemed not to know what to do about it. And the blood was all the more confusing to her. She seemed to not know what that moisture meant when she felt it on her clothing.

Then, in a wave of intuition, I realized that this girl was experiencing embarrassment. Oh, not just for her being in heat. But it was as if she had never before felt embarrassment before at all. Not ever. And that, curiously, she had never been in heat before. And the feeling spun around her head in gusts of confusion. She did not even know what this feeling might be called. It was in that forceful way, completely unknown to her. But she felt confused and giddy and her senses raced and crashed about her body. It was as if she had never felt this sensation, of this uncomfortable combination of shame and mortification, flustered and jittery and she did not know why. Then she looked around for the ar-dist and, seeing him, felt worse. Now she was humiliated, self-doubting. Apparently these were feelings she had never felt before. I could almost swear to it, but we canines rarely feel the need to swear to anything.

Odd, all of this.

Most females that our ar-dist brought to the studio were chatty and independent and show-offy and they readily approached him with mating behaviors that were at once practiced and alluring.

And as human beings, and as animals, they did what had to be done, with sudden urgency, then, with sudden exhaustion, these females would fall asleep. So, too, my ar-dist.

This girlfriend was different. Not even a girl. And certainly not a friend. I puzzled over this.

Then, after a peculiar adumbrated conversation between this odd female presence and our ar-dist, he fled the studio, slamming the door behind himself. Angry, I think. But slamming the door, now he was gone.

5

At this gesture, this girl, or friend, or neither, but certainly not both, spoke:

"This is so damned hard. I had no idea how hard this would be. And what's this mess I have made? I bleed, well they all do that, I knew that. But it is happening — I had no idea how, how, how — how this would feel."

She cried. Well, that's what girlfriends do. At least that part was recognizable, common to girlfriends. But it did not feel the same somehow. My fur stood back up again and I started to swirl around again and, spinning fast, I skidded sideways and dramatically threw up my dinner. What was going on here?

Then I watched her stumble over to the bed and she lay down on the sheets and curled her legs close to her chest and listened to her own heart beating. And cried real human tears:

"I cannot do this thing. I love this man. I hate this loving thing."

I sensed that she was suddenly reminded that on special occasions angels may assume the shape of men or of animals. Puzzling, that.

"It is so much harder than I thought it was going to be. I cannot do this thing. I should never have desired to be a human being. Foolish girl. I begged for it. Foolish girl."

I had seen and heard regret many times by now in my puppy life. It is in the nature of a dog to comfort — we cannot help it. Even to comfort a person who does not deserve to be comforted. It is in our natures. My canine duty overwhelmed my confusion and fears of this girl, this friend, this girlfriend, neither girl nor friend. I jumped up on the mattress and lay down beside her back and stretched out all four of my legs and pressed my warm paw pads against her icy spine and along her shivering ribcage and began to sense that she was sleeping now. Despite my own fearful anguish, I believe that I provided comfort to her, canine comfort, to ease her anguish. She fell off to sleep. As did I.

The following morning, this strange girl prepares to leave us.

As I mentioned, in her own language, our cat speaks clearly to this girl as she twists the doorknob, opens the door a few inches, and steps a foot outside the threshold. We hear this poor diminished girl say, quite clearly as she leaves us:

"Why did I ever do this thing?"

Then she turns around for just a moment to take a long last look into the studio. As she turns, she sees the cat and the cat speaks directly to her, quite clearly, in her own foreign tongue. It sounded like this to my canine ears, but I may be wrong:

"Tu es folle ma petite."

Not being conversant in the cat's native tongue, as I said, I do not know what her words might signify. Perhaps the cat wished this strange girl well as she takes leave of our studio and of our ar-dist and of our lives.

The cat and I reside in parallel galaxies, stars bright, each one of us, but never inhabiting the same atmosphere. We stand this time, side by side, and feel the dimming of the strange atmosphere as the girl walks down the stairs and back into her own corporeal world again. I do believe she needs, beyond rationality, to contemplate her human self. She might discover something useful and I wish her well. However, I intuit that getting back may prove very daunting for her.

The cat and I both know that angels may assume the shape of animals. Of animals, too, that's right, and so it is believed. The cat and I sit side by side in agreement on this last, at last.

Hannah-Naomi

1

I fled Gershom's studio. I was insane. Stupid. Stupid. Drugged on passion. Brain damaged. Couldn't care less if I had abandoned my duties as Guardian Angel to Artemisia. To hell with being a Guardian Angel. All I desired was to lie with this man, Gershom Holder. To be his lover. Nothing could stop me. This was, of course, perverse. In irrationally leaving my status as a Guardian Angel, I instantly became both a human being and Fallen Angel. And this: this was love? Well, so I believed.

"But Mother: I LUV him."

I had heard this all before, tens of thousands of times. But what it felt like, I never knew.

Then, intrusively ringing in my ears, came the words of the Creation Director. It was quite clear that my passion for love put me in ". . . a desecration of your responsibilities of guardianship" and that my so-called need for human love was "near to blasphemous . . ."

The Creation Director had also reminded me that:

"You have been seduced by a son of men . . . This is very dangerous ground. This is not love. This is a seduction. You are nothing to this son of men . . . You are about to turn your world upside-down. Not to mention, you will turn the world of Artemisia, with whom you have been tasked with a lifetime of guardianship, you will most certainly turn her world upside-down along with your own."

I did not care. I wanted Gershom.

Our new relationship, such as it was now, had been completely at my whim. In my new skin as a human woman, I was baffled by every single thing. And, having relinquished my Guardian Angel tool kit, I could not make head nor tails of what was going on inside Gershom's mind. His soul was locked safely away from any intrusions I would have had if I had become his Guardian Angel.

Well what had I expected?

How delusional I had become as a human woman. What fantasies I had. But much had been taken from me. I was no longer a Guardian Angel, but I was an adversary of Gershom Holder's. Interacting with him now in my incarnation as a stupid, selfish, inexperienced little human girl, well, at the very least he must see me as ridiculous.

Why had he been so upset with me? He actually slammed the door as he left. In a huff. How could he have left me alone in his studio? Alone. Well, not quite. I had the company of his dog and his cat. They had seemed to like me. They had been curious and somewhat attentive. I was humiliated. What had just happened I wondered? Why was I bleeding? Was I injured? Nobody had prepared me for blood. Was this a trick from the Creation Director? A test? Something to send me screaming back to my guardianship duties?

2

As I walked along a noisy bad smelling street, jammed with angry drivers and argumentative passengers, I started thinking, devising a strategy: could I return to Guardian Angel status? Surely it would not be easy. I was already in much trouble in that department. But perhaps I could re-connect with the Gig Economy and thus bypass the ire of the Creation Director? I must try at least. I am a mess. I cannot do this thing. Why on earth would I have ever desired to be a human being, a female no less? Why? I had no idea what the cat had said to me as I was leaving the studio. But maybe she was right when she said to me:

"Le cœur a ses raisons que la raison ne connat point. Allez ma petite."

I will need to look it up some day. But meanwhile, I needed more urgently however, to meet with the Creation Director. I'll be angelic and humble and desperate. I needed help.

No!

Do not seek the help of the Creation Director. That would be like in the olden times when Guardian Angels had to get permission and assistance for every single thing they did. I had already discovered that we do posses an element of independence, of self-determination, an ability for Freethinking.

Maybe I will just return to Gershom's studio. Maybe I could make this thing work.

3

I return.

He is silent.

This is love?

It is love.

Is this love?

I do not know.

We sit.

I fasten onto his gaze. He withholds himself. It's that old trick of his. I don't know how to approach this creature.

He rises.

He saunters over to his canvas, swings it deftly onto the work table, takes up a can of paint and a brush and starts to paint. I have no earthly idea of what he is painting. A dog?

He picks up his battered pack of Camels. Teases out a rather crushed remnant of a cigarette, lights up with a flick and spits off a puff of smoke overhead. Ah, the seduction of the silent artist wielding his tools: his paints, his brushes, his cigarette. The moves. The seeming indifference to my presence. It is certain madness, is it not? I am drawn into his smoky orbit. Put the paintbrush down.

4

I had already fallen. In love? It could be debated. And now, finally, I anticipated floating. Being embraced. Being transported. Being engulfed by my Very Great Love in passionate resonance, just us two, in a loving tangle. I placed my hand over his hand, engaged as it was, in painting. Working? I could not tell. He looked at and moved brushes on the canvas. On his picture. Enough of that. Let's get on with it.

I said: "Stop. Look at me."

And he did. Coolly. Not exactly with eyes that registered passion. Not precisely if at all. But what did I know of such expressions? Having never seen nor received such glances, having always been on the outside, a mere observer of these human passions, as an observer, as a mere Guardian Angel. Now that I had been transformed into a human woman, I was utterly lacking in knowledge, intuition, or just plain experience — lacking all of this, thus I did not recognize passion in my own body, nor in the nearness of my own Very Great Love — the now incomprehensible Gershom Holder. I was bereft of my Guardian Angel Portfolio of Tools. Now I was just a girl. Looking what I hoped would be meaningfully, into the eyes of one of the sons of men. And I had no earthly idea of what to expect. No earthly idea of what this was supposed to feel like. And *earthly* is the operative word here: now that I was a creature of the earth, I was helpless. Ignorant. Unprepared. As a former Guardian Angel, I might have nudged any one of my charges and advised something along the line of: Be mysterious.

I start to babble. How about a bit of small talk?:

"You have no idea how much I have anticipated this, our being together in the same room at last warming to your embrace, anticipating your lips on mine, and your arms embracing, er, my body."

No.

That did not sound right. Too many words. Too quickly recited. Not enough passion.

This was not working.

Maybe if I spoke more I could propel action from him:

"Don't you at least want to know who I really am? I mean, here I appear out of nowhere and aren't you at least curious to know how I got to be here what, for instance, are my dearest hopes, dreams, and aspirations."

This was babbling. I hear myself. These are not words of passion to induce passion in my Very Great Love. However, I continue:

"Your paintings are fantastic and so many of them and all of animals or of dogs or maybe they are sprites and the colors fantastical. I have been inside many important museums and many important gallery openings, with many important artists."

This is met with silence. My Very Great Love is silent. This is not going well.

5

I shout:

"Gershom! Did you hear me? Are you listening to me? Ger! Ger?"

My Very Great Love looks away. Very Great Love. Supposedly. Saying nothing in response, he re-lights his cigarette and puffs hard his smoke, upwards, and now, squinting, he looks in my direction and his voice echoes in the large studio as he shouts:

"Do. Not. Call. Me. Ger."

That's it?

He shouts at me? I shout back:

"Get a grip, Ger!

6

I cannot do this thing. Lost is all. Neither fish nor fowl, but foul, indeed. I fall. Fallen Angel, I fall farther. I am in free fall, legs flung up in the air, torso folded, arms flailing, wingless. My world turns upside-down. I flee. Words fail.

CHAVA

1

WHAT ARE YOU DOING HERE Hannah-Naomi?

I realize — too late, maybe. I must sound like a lunatic. I mean, here I am asking Hannah-Naomi somewhat logical questions having to do with memory retrieval, or with her being a Fallen Angel, or with her own insights into — into what? The bottom line here is that I am speaking with a Guardian Angel. This alone is suspect. This alone indicts my sanity. But I have more and urgent questions for you Hannah-Naomi:

Why are you telling me about your Very Great Love? Supposed. Why have you chosen me to tell your story to? What am I supposed to do for you?

I am baffled. Confused.

Words fail.

Hannah-Naomi

1

Well phooey on him. I can live without my Very Great Love — without Gershom Holder. Lots of human women do so, and nary bat an eyelash. I figure I can take care of myself. I have done so before. I do not require attentions from my Very Great Love. Nor support. I can take care of myself. I'll go out on my own and get a job. An apartment. I will get a VISA. I'll get a job as an advertising copywriter. Back in the day, I was a Guardian Angel to several of those types. And, after all, I am writing a book aren't I and I already know quite a bit about market segmentation, and product branding, and suchlike. My book includes much in it about my Fall from grace as a Guardian Angel. Very heady stuff, especially for the doubters. Little do they know that I certainly do have experience doing gig work as a Guardian Angel prior to my fall and where better to get gigs than at an advertising agency. I mean no disrespect, but being a Guardian Angel well prepares a soul to work in a soulless industry. Thus, I am perfectly well suited to seek work as an advertising copywriter. And now that I am a Fallen Angel, there is a certain cachet that attaches to my transformation from Guardian Angel into Fallen Angel which I can attach to my resume. This kind of backstory will enhance my qualifications. This kind of branding will do me nothing but good as it places me among the "characters" and the "stars". I will join the glitterati in the upper echelons of the advertising biz. See. I already know the jargon. What could be more heaven-sent, than my transformation into an advertising copywriter. I wouldn't just sell my grandmother. It is always a question of "for how much? After all: I bailed on both of my Guardian Angel charges, tossing them to one side as I begged to become a human female and to be relieved of my duties as a Guardian Angel. If I could do that, I would be very well suited to being in the ad biz.

They're going to love me. I will even have a secretary! Will wonders never cease. I am ready to take on any challenge when I hear the call:

"Be an angel and bring me a cup of coffee."

I can do this.

By that time, I, your Guardian Angel, I had already abandoned both Gershom Holder and Artemisia Gershom for my own, and new, mortal passions. I got a gig at a big ad agency. Advertising Copywriter. Right up my alley, strewn with cliches. I can do this. Nothing like a little commerce to interrupt a clear view of reality. Like how I abandoned my duties as a Guardian Angel. Went off the rails in love with one of the sons of men. Oh well. Off I went into the wild blue yonder of dog food and fast food and interest-bearing savings accounts.

With my dubious ethics, I am made for these things!

2

Again, with no transition, I find myself fully ensconced at a large ad agency, reporting to a Vice President Creative Group Head, a woman no less, one of the first human females to occupy that title in this rarefied corporate battleground. It's Artemisia Gershom. This is too close for comfort. Yet, she has certainly changed since I abandoned her guardianship.

Redhead, cigarette-smoker, chic plum suede pumps, two hundred dollars a foot, businesslike lunch-drinker, she taps the rim of her empty martini glass with a single glossy nail and the waiter flies over to the table with:

"Refresh your drinks ladies?"

Refills arrive, brimful, olives, dry, very dry, ahhhh.

She looks into my face; appraising. Will I be her competitor? Will I need a push? Can I write copy, for-godssake? Copy, fast, to deadline? Copy, clever? After all. If I can do that task I might make her look good to the corner office on her determined trudge up to the next title.

"And so, Hannah-Naomi, this evening we're doing a focus group for the dog food placements. You have, I assume, reviewed the market segmentation and some of the latest research in your notebook?"

I have done.

And again, without a seeming transition, I find myself situated in a small dark room adjacent to a large conference room that is filling with average consumers. Our little room is hidden behind a large mirror and women come up to the mirror to straighten an eyebrow or twist a lock of errant hair. Or, tongue out, a guy breathes into his palm, breath okay. Big surprise; it's a mirror. We nestle behind it so we may observe the activities in the big room. As if any of those consumers really thinks this is an ordinary mirror, not a see-through device to watch your average dog owner as they sniff open cans of product.

Today's marketing exercise is called a cutting.

With a dramatic flourish, trays of open cans of dog food are brought in by the moderator's assistant. The can labels are removed and each one has a coded letter and numeral so that only the moderator knows which is which.

Astoundingly to me — who has never viewed this variety of human activity — ordinary consumers pass along each can, hand to hand, inhale sniffs, and they either nod appreciatively or scrunch up a nose in disgust and say:

"Ewwww. Rover just hates this kind."

Or, better:

"Fido would just love this one!"

Frankly I found this whole display of human ego and vanity to be appalling. Worse, with all the snuffling at the edges of open cans of dog food, it was disgusting. Who says their dog loves or hates a smelly dog food? Why not give real dogs real samples of each food? What kind of market research is this? Who cares if the human being who owns a dog likes a certain aroma? Or stench as the case may be. And who says a human being OWNS a dog? Really! And it will be my job to write an ad that will please the scent glands of a human being. Or am I to write an ad that would appeal to an actual DOG? Should I write my copy in dog language? If so, how? This ad biz is more complicated, with its own absurdities and sub-rosa agendas than I might have ever imagined. I'm so confused.

Before this puzzlement gets any worse, I am asking my Creative Group Head if we can meet after hours to discuss. She is always up for drinkies after work in what everyone refers to as The Downstairs Conference Room, a dingy rat-infested bar.

"Okay, see you then. I pencil in her name on the bottom of today's page of my calendar: Meeting, Artemisia, 7:00 pm. Downstairs."

3

"You know, Hannah-Naomi," she says, "you look familiar to me."

"Oh? Yeah?"

Careful, I do not care to reveal to her anything that could be interpreted by her as more revealing.

"No. I mean it. Did you ever work on the Bunny Butter account about ten years ago back east?"

"Um, well, no. This is my first copywriting gig."

"Hmmm. Odd. You just seem so familiar."

At this, Artemisia takes a long sip of her requisite martini, swizzles it around her mouth as if she were rinsing her teeth of burger bits.

"So. You wanted to talk to me about something?"

"Yes. Yes, I am puzzled about the dog food research. Especially the consumer insights, so-called, gained in the cutting session. Focus group. Whatever it is. And I am baffled at why the samples of dog food were offered to human beings. Instead of dogs. You see."

Artemisia squints, silently appraising me as I speak.

"I mean. What I mean is, who is the consumer of this dog food? I mean. Am I writing an ad to those people from that room? Those so called consumers, snuffling and mumbling into open cans of dog food? But, I hesitate. Shouldn't I, rather, direct my copy — target, tone and manner, and all that — to our real prospect: a dog? Don't you see?"

Artemisia hawks a deep cigarette smoker's laugh/cough. She really is amused and says to me:

"Well, then Hannah-Naomi. Go ahead. Do it that way. Talk to your consumer: a dog. See if you can. You're right of course. So now sit down at your typewriter and talk dog. Do that ad in Dog Talk. See if you can."

And with that, her lovely first finger slipped, lovingly, around the rim of her empty martini glass and the waiter appears out of thin air with a fresh one. He, a well-trained dog. Waiter.

"So tell me Hannah-Naomi: do you have a full-time boyfriend. Or other: fill in the blank."

"Well it's funny you ask, Artemisia, there was just one Very Great Love. But to tell you the truth, I was worlds more impressed with his dog. And the dog to me. I think. Maybe that's why I wonder more about doing my ad copy directed at a dog. I know dogs. I relate to dogs. Maybe, in another incarnation, I was a dog."

This was getting too close for comfort. Pretty soon I'll be suggesting to Artemisia that dogs could be Guardian Angels. I better not go there.

"Actually my Very Great Love and I split up recently. Hence me looking for copywriting gigs. And, happily, found you. Found this one."

"You know Hannah-Naomi, you and I must have been friends in another life. Yes? I mean that. You and I have a certain similar world view, for lack of a better word. And you do seem so familiar. Like it's Deja Vu or some such. You think?"

"Ah yes. Here's to advertising, market segmentation, product placement, the whole darn thing. Woof!"

4

"You did it Hannah-Naomi. Here's to Hannah-Naomi, Copywriter Extraordinaire — all caps — gone straight to the dogs."

Artemisia raises her glass to the room. All hail, me, Hannah-Naomi.

A nice handful of my colleagues raise their glasses and raise a minor ruckus, cheering, and jeering, my work, all in celebration of my award-winning dog food campaign. Talking directly to dogs. Gone quite willfully, happily even, going straight to the dogs, I am.

My campaign was so quirky, so elegant in its way, with a headline that read:

> **This Dogfood Goes To the Dogs** — and a funny TV commercial with the print copy of the ad under the dog bowl and an adorable mutt who sniffs and snuffles the newspaper under his bowl. You had to be there. The shoot was a riot. Try, just try, to get a series of dogs to look under their bowls. Our hero dog did a masterful job.

I must say: it all went to my head. Never had I ever presided over such a successful enterprise. Never mind during my former incarnation as Guardian Angel. Never. The accolades poured in. And money, of course. I got a hefty raise and a new office with three big south-facing window panels. And a door. With a lock. I had arrived. Or, rather, I was enroute to arrival. Part of all this, of course, was the support I got from my Creative Group Head, Vice President of course, Artemisia Gershom.

Yet there was a peculiar disconnect in our relationship. Well, of course. From my perspective as her former Guardian Angel, it was obvious. But what I was picking up on was something more important. Artemisia was disconnected. She was not really there. She had no there there. It was particularly evident when I was hanging out with her at the Downstairs Conference Room, evenings after work. She was there and yet not fully engaged.

How do I know this? It is most likely the residual of a bit of my former skills as a Guardian Angel — the ability to read souls, if that is not too grand. How about this: it is my intuition based upon seeing and hearing a human being seated across the table in this dim watering hole, glasses half full.

Some human beings have this skill — the ability to discern people's inner workings, for lack of a better description. Some people can glean a person's character from a single glance. Yet, sadly, other people do not have that ability. To see into a person, a human being who is otherwise separate from another human being, that instantaneous assessment of one person by another person, a stranger outside another stranger's skin, it is not a universal gift as in the gift of eyesight, hearing, or being left-handed. In the case of quick and accurate assessment of one person by another, I like to call it "bullshit detection". Having accurate and active bullshit detection is a very great, immensely useful skill. In my case, it is the only residual skill, a thin strand of this ability to assess a stranger sitting here with me in my human incarnation. It is about the only thing left over from my Guardian Angel Portfolio, my bag of tricks, my useful tools that I turned to when I was a Guardian Angel. And what I see now before me is my former charge, ensconced in her place in the corporeal and corporate world. She is functioning very well. But there is something missing and that is her heartbeat, so to speak. More accurately, metaphorically, she has lost heart. She really does not connect to her current successes with deep personal conviction or satisfaction.

Her elegant finger glides around the rim of her empty martini glass. Our waiter heaves to with our next round. And that is it for Artemisia.

"So, Artemisia — do you believe in Guardian Angels?"

She glares at me over the rim of her martini. With a ladylike snort, she shoots back:

"You mean like my mother taught me as in when her repeated words: "Remember, Artemisia, you have a Guardian Angel." Like that Hannah-Naomi? You've got to be kidding."

"Well. Just curious."

"Well, Hannah-Naomi, I do have a keen bullshit detector. If that equates with having a Guardian Angel I'm with you. Would you say that a Guardian Angel can take the form of a Keen Bullshit Detector?"

I am fidgeting now. This is getting a bit too close for comfort.

We each take a sip of our elixirs. Artemisia runs her tongue around the rim of her glass, relaxes into telling me about an episode in her experience:

"Here's an example of mine. My Keen Bullshit Detector. A while back we got a new client. After the handshakes and first input meeting I reported back down the hallway to management: this will be COD. Management was appalled. Our agency had never made such a proviso. I was adamant however. COD it was. Thus we got a payment at three points during the deliverables before moving on to each subsequent portion of the project. When it was time for the printing — it had morphed into a huge full color promo package — I warned our printing rep:

"Better do COD."

He said to me:

"Don't worry Missy. We're big boys."

"Just sayin' Buddy-boy."

"So what happened, Artemisia?"

"Printer was stiffed. Surprise, surprise."

Another restorative sip of martini.

"Printer got stiffed. Our creative department in our agency got paid, however. COD nice and proper. Thank you very much to my personal Bullshit Detector. It was that client. All hail fellow, well met, plenty of har har har. It was his Piaget watch that set off my trusty Bullshit Detector. COD. I was right. Bless my Guardian Angelic very keen Bullshit Detector."

5

Well, so things, career-wise, were going swimmingly for both Artemisia and for me, her brilliant hire. We clicked along with award after award. Always, of course, her name came first on the statuettes of honor, then mine. Never mind. It's the way of the 'team', quote unquote. It's always 'credit goes to the team' when everybody knows, full and well, and precisely, who, which single one of us, came up with the winning headline, concept, layout. Yet, the ads slide gracefully into the enormous portfolios we carried back in those days, especially when out on the street, seeking a new, or better, or existent, job. Well, in the uncanny way that management views these portfolios during job interviews — in that bit of psychic evaluation of a copywriter's work — even management knows full and well who actually wrote the ads. I would say that the best of the management ranks actually are blessed with very fine, very accurate, bullshit detectors.

Ah, well.

But such are the ways of the ad biz that, sooner rather than later, a hefty client flees the agency of record and the shit hits the fan. Excrement, rather, launches skyward. And sooner, rather than later, someone creeps into my office, surreptitiously closes the door, and says to me:

"Guess what?"

"What?" I say, dumbfoundment oozing from my expression.

"We've lost the XYZ account. Client up and left. Big changes coming, mark my words. Don't say anything to anybody about this. It hasn't been formally announced. Not a word."

Oh do not worry. I am skilled at keeping secrets. So-called. But I know inevitably, by close of day, another person will rinse and repeat the ceremony of the secret, just between thee and me, with the caution:

"Don't tell anybody."

I know. I know. Cross my heart.

And what I also know, full and well, is that blood will be shed. Heads will roll. Sooner, rather than later, moments after the formal announcement of the departure of this major client.

We find ourselves, we survivors, we few, gathered, desolate but cheerfully still alive — clutching our lifeboats filled with vodka or three fingers of Scotch — and our conversation, here in this benighted watering hole, is that of subdued ecstasy at the fact that is has not been one of us. Rather, it has been one of our former best friends on staff, colleagues, team-mates. It was someone else who heard:

"What have you done for us lately?"

They tote their box of personal affects down to the parking garage. Poor them. Lucky us.

In something of an ill-fated alcoholic stupor, I start to expound:

"Wow. What a bit of luck," I say, slurring unguardedly.

Artemisia taps out her rather longish ash, into a little glass dish with the imprint: *Los Angeles Angelus Bar.*

"You think so, Hannah-Naomi?"

"Well. Yes. Of course. Don't you?"

"Well, Hannah-Naomi, sooner rather than later that will be you — or me — toting our keepsakes down to the garage. The detritus of our careers. It will happen. Down we'll go. Mark, as they say, my words."

"Yes, but Artemisia, you're still here. I'm still here. Isn't that good?"

Artemisia coughs a not very cheery laugh.

"You think so, Hannah-Naomi?"

"Well, yes. I do."

"Well, let me inform you of your naiveté, Hannah-Naomi. You are sadly wrong. Just stupidly, I mean no disrespect of you, you are just stupid to believe you will escape the shit as it careens around your head and you pack up your little keepsakes and off you go, portfolio in hand, off to the head-hunters.

"But, we were saved, Artemisia."

Artemisia chokes. What follows is a loud coughing fit, spilling of her half empty martini glass into the popcorn basket, a dramatic rescue by our dedicated waiter, whisking up the flooded popcorn, wiping the table.

"You want me to believe some hokum about Guardian Angels? Do you Hannah-Naomi?"

"Well, yes. Maybe. I don't know. We were saved today weren't we? Don't you believe in Guardian Angels then, Artemisia?"

"No. Not when I hear bullshit like this:

"Well, you were always there. What have you done for us lately?"

Artemisia taps the rim of her martini glass with the blue sapphire ring of her elegantly manicured middle finger — the finger with which you flip people off. Our waiter swings over to our table. Smoothly, swiftly he places the polished, replenished glass, front and center, to Artemisia. Seamlessly, he makes the old empty disappear.

What I learned, somewhat haphazardly and perhaps way too late to be of assistance, was all about the world of my former charge, Artemisia Gershom. I learned of, and witnessed, her numb irony that had piled higher and deeper so as to completely block off who she had the potential to be. And she did not even realize it. Artemisia was all but obliterated. Her artist self was surely dead. Certainly that. This is what had become of her after I fell in love with one of the sons of men and fled into human womanhood, leaving Artemisia on her own, about to graduate from college, without a Guardian Angel.

Perfect: she pursues a career in a line of business that repeats the same words that she has heard echoing in her soul for decades:

"You were always there. What have you done for us lately?"

6

And I GOT it then: Artemisia's very choice of livelihood, recreates the pivotal words that the world had already handed to her, earlier in life:

Gossip.

Words. But words cannot kill you. Come on, Artemisia. Buck up. Let's get going.

And that, dear reader, finishes my foray into a dim past. Artemisia was a scoffer. I was a Fallen Angel. I had fallen, all right, straight into the world of money-making, career-clutching clichés. The ways of the corporeal — or should I rather say, the corporate world — were, or had been for me, intensely attractive and, as it turned out, devastatingly vain. This is how Artemisia had existed after I had relinquished my duties to her as her Guardian Angel.

Chava

1

Hannah-Naomi leans forward on her chair, head in hands. Her gesture is similar to a human gesture, as if she were about to cry or to shout tearful regrets. But I do believe that that kind of anguish is not possible in a Guardian Angel. Without human vulnerabilities, she could not be able to cry out in anger nor in despair nor in shame. Right here in my studio, now filled with morning sunshine, Hannah-Naomi is experiencing something deeply shaming, but she cannot react in an angelic way. She must have needed this catharsis of her own cathexis. But why here? Why now? And why with me? Why is she unburdening herself here with me? Why perform her confession with me as her witness? With me, a single human being at this singular moment? I do not know. Is a puzzlement. Is it she or is it I who are becoming increasingly discombobulated? Something is off. I cannot say exactly what. But I know something is wrong with this visit and with my visitor, Hannah-Naomi.

Hannah-Naomi

1

Seeing my failure in my Guardianship of Artemisia, I began to feel all-too-human guilt. I had a vague notion that if I could return to my Guardian Angel status that I could fix things in Artemisia's life.

It was time for me, Hannah-Naomi, to try, I mean to really try to ingratiate myself back with the Creation Director. To reinstate myself to my former Guardian Angel status. And not just for myself: for Artemisia. To see if I could reconcile my Fallen Angel persona and to return to the duties, the responsibilities, of being her Guardian Angel. Gig worker or not, I must do this.

What I discovered during my foray into being a human being — in addition to the force of passion for my Very Great Love, I had dabbled in the world of other human passions — for money, for fame, for fellow-feeling, kudos. For martinis. And not unlike my failure to wrap things up with my Very Great Love, I fell back on the lure of other human desires. Yet, I came to see, in human terms, how I had failed to guide and prod and build up my charge and how deeply I had failed her. Not to mention my worst failing: I had abandoned her. I also had relinquished even the faintest possibility of becoming Guardian Angel for Gershom Holder. Ah, yes. My Very Great Love. Former. I had failed them both — Artemisia and Gershom. Neither fish nor fowl, but definitely foul — I was a mess.

Enough! I must meet again with the Creation Director.

2

After leaving my employ as an Advertising Copywriter and after ingratiating myself with the Creation Director, I was deemed worthy enough to be reinstated, within limits, to my role as a Guardian Angel. Not yet to be returned to my Gig Guardian Angel status, but close enough to start to work again in my former angelic capacities — along with my Guardian Angel Portfolio with its tools of my trade.

What I discovered as I returned to Artemisia was this:

It had been eleven years since Artemisia had painted anything:

The studio smells of ink. Slide, thump, bang, bang. Squeegees sliding swiftly over silk. Thump into their frame. The running ink settles onto the bottom of the frame, one color at a time, a viscous puddle of yellow.

Then black. For decades this serigraph, created by Artemisia Gershom, this serigraph will reside, flat, inside its battered black portfolio, tied along the edges with frayed black strings, leaning against a leaky sub-basement wall. Forgotten, this serigraph will later be remembered, retranscribed. It is nearly ruined now, moldy in its battered hideaway. This last work of art, this serigraph created by Artemisia — the remaining evidence of someone the artist — Artemisia — could only dimly recall.

"Was that artist me?" Artemisia, asks herself, "Who created this thing? This object? Why is it still here? Is it still here?"

Slide. Thump. Bang. There is an echo: what an odd memory. No, Artemisia had not thought about this for a very long time. The sounds of serigraphy fade in fugue. Yet hiding. Her world was turned upside-down. Then black. Then nothing. No thing. She was still alive however.

> *"It takes a lot of time to be a genius, you have to sit around so much doing nothing, really doing nothing." — Gertrude Stein*

3

Did Artemisia notice that her Guardian Angel had left her? Did she even think in those terms: that of having her very own Guardian Angel?

No.

She did not.

No.

She did not think in those terms. That her Guardian Angel had disappeared, had left, abandoned her. She never once thought that the abandonment of her Guardian Angel had caused her mother to die. Does that mean that Artemisia did not believe in Guardian Angels back then?

Discovering her old serigraph, a decade later, Artemisia discovered the significance of a memory of just five small words that had put an abrupt halt to any delusions she may have had to becoming an artist. How ridiculous. Her desire to paint. How lacking in self awareness not to have known how much she had gone numb. Ridiculous. But just a few words put the brakes on her creativity, yet left intact in her brain or whatever you want to call it — left in one piece was her practical little self, the will and ability to survive, to live on. Artemisia strode out into the world, with energetic self-confidence and got the first of several jobs. She needed to live and to live meant to make a living. Funny how live is the antecedent, the prefix, to the word living.

4

It's time. Now for something important. It is time to shift into the buried consciousness of Artemisia Gershom. If I am to return back to my being a standard issue Guardian Angel, I must press on, using the best of my Portfolio of Tricks of my former trade.

It is time for Memory Work.

Artemisia needs to see again a painful memory. To retranscribe this event if possible, years after it took place. She needs to finally **get** what it meant.

Here, Artemisia. Look:

It is this: Gossip. That is a noun meaning one who speaks the words of gossip. Gossiping, the verb.

It would be years, a bit over a decade, before Artemisia ***gets*** what was about to transpire between her and this woman, the gossip, noun. She possessed quite an aggregation of points of gossip, plural, nouns. She had a lot to lay out to Artemisia.

She nabbed Artemisia at a subdued little holiday gathering held at Artemisia's home, her mother's house, just a few days after Artemisia's mother's funeral. A gossip, singular, co-opted Artemisia from the other guests for a little chinwag — just us girls.

What kind of person, that girl-friend — neither girl nor friend — makes you sit down for what would become a bruising tete-à-tete? What kind of person, her face just shy of needing what women euphemistically refer to as: *work*. She arranged for an office procedure to enhance or revise her formerly youthful chin, lift those droopy eyelids, lubricate, once more, her full and youthful lips, to transform her face again into pretty and better do it pretty soon, you, the gossip. Noun.

At this point, now overdue for those procedures, this gossip sits Artemisia down in her mother's own living room, where she, Artemisia, had grown up. This gossip plunks Artemisia down on one of her mother's favorite upholstered chairs, nice and comfy and chummy and with practiced casual viciousness disguised as humid familiarity, this woman, this stranger, a gossip, has to tell Artemisia things about her former family. She embellishes her monologue with details and informs Artemesia, just between us girls, of things Artemesia should never have had to hear. And, as if that were not enough, Artemisia sees through a haze of disbelief that that woman, that gossip, is wearing one of Artemisia's dresses. A dress she had made herself, senior year of college. Simplicity Pattern.

She tells Artemisia things she thinks Artemisia needs to know.

She has deft access to gutter phrases, the coded language, murmured, confidential and suggestive. She is accustomed to saying these kinds of words clearly enough and just loud enough to penetrate past the rolled-down driver's side car window.

And, now, as if to emphasize her role, she is wearing one of Artemisia's dresses, that she took, or was instructed to wear, from the closet in what used to be Artemisia's old bedroom, upstairs from this, Artemisia's own living room. Former.

What kind of person is that, that gossip?

Oh, sure. People have suffered worse. God. Living in this world is a cruel endeavor. Yet, that day, during this woman's enforced gabfest with Artemesia, she staked her claim to the living room, the bedrooms, and to the entire house and its contents. Artemisia's home. Former.

"Get your hands off my mother's things. Take that dress off."

5

That woman, that gossip, wanted to preempt all other claimants in attendance at this holiday gathering. With a guise of frankness, oily sincerity, she laid bare her gossip. Right there in your mother's living room. Not hers. Not yours either, Artemisia. Not any more.

With her gossip, her perverted heart-to-heart, she desecrates cherished memories — former — leaves them shattered, obliterated.

"And what, pray tell," the gossip asks Artemisia, "what did you think he did on all those business trips out of town?"

Artemisia could not stop up her ears. And she discovered that, apparently, nothing in her little life, up to that moment, listening to this gossip, had been at all what it had seemed to be to her.

Nor would it ever be the same again.

And then, as if that had not been bad enough, this gossip reloaded, cocked, and took aim, point blank, at what was left of Artemisia's confused heart:

"And do you know what he said about you?"

"What do you mean?"

"About you, little goody two shoes. You, sitting here in this fancy house. But let me tell you something. I asked him how come he never did all the exciting things, the heroic things, that were meant to crown his life. And how come he never went back to Europe to travel, to dine with fine wines, to get a red sportscar. You know. Midlife crisis stuff. And you know what he said? He said because YOU were always there. Your needs put his life on hold, postponed every, single, thing in his life. Braces on your teeth. Dresses and shoes for school. A fancy college education, bought and paid for by him with his hard, boring, snorting, ass-kissing climb up the corporate ladder. And always for you. And you know what he always said? He always said to me that it was all because:

"You were always there. And what had you ever done for him lately?"

Artemisia's memory of this event, reviewed through memory work at the nudge of me, her Guardian Angel, it was mere gossip, but powerful.

BANG.

Artemisia's life changed.

BANG.

Words can kill.

And the door to her creativity slammed shut. Killed as if by bullets. Artemisia the artist was dead.

It would take decades to percolate into her comprehension of what, exactly, had happened that day. That memory of gossip, mere, would take years before it could be retranscribed into meaning and after meaning was discovered, it would take more decades for her to act.

Sadly, and also part of this memory Artemisia, is this: that gossip slammed into you during the period of time when I had abandoned you, when I had given up my Guardian Angel status with you, one of my charges, and was gone from you, out and about in the mortal world, being a woman in pursuit of my Very Great Love, Gershom Holder. Very sadly, you were without my assistance on that day. I was at that point a Fallen Angel. You were alone in the world to hear, and later to bear, the poison words of that gossip.

Meanwhile, you did your thing: when in doubt, do nothing. But do not forget, Artemisia. Never forget. You never did forget that bit of gossip. It very nearly killed you. It killed your aspirations, your confidence, your self as an artist. The artist in you was made mute by words of gossip. That gossip, and its memory, were muffled, yet that gossip spoke to the power of words to do very great harm.

But no: it did not kill, however, your ability to survive. That, you retained, intact, bitter though it was. But the best part of your self and soul was deadened. They call it fugue. Such a lovely sounding word. But dark, stunted, disaffected. Seeing this in you, I knew that with or without my assistance as your Guardian Angel, you would need to learn how to draw upon your experiences, even very bitter ones, in order for you to survive and even, perhaps, to thrive. As you strive to become an artist, you will eventually learn how to draw upon even these painful memories.

Listen, Artemisia. This is what happened to you from gossip: These were mistakes that gossip committed before you with evil inclination.

6

Flying, Falling, Floating — as if death were not enough, you lost your home, whole rooms — living, dining, library, den, bedrooms, bathrooms — and every single thing within them, small objects — kitchen spoons, the glass by the bedside, books and books and books, and pictures, and a souvenir stone from a beach — and yet more, even, was lost as well. Your whole family, whole memories, the very abiding concept of what you had believed had been your own past, the love and affection and protection of your family — now former and forever after, that family would remain for you *former* — all of these were shattered, shattered into shards, broken memories lodged inside your heart, Artemisia. Destroyed by gossip. Much of it due to that gossip, noun. Some of it due to an accretion of thoughtless spoken words, uttered over decades, shuffled between ear and heart. Not forgotten. Yet, active, years after utterance.

Buy, hey: these are only words.

So what?

Words can't kill you. Right?

7

I saw and heard the effects of words on both of my charges. Both Gershom and Artemisia had the acute hearing of childhood to hear and to absorb hurtful words clearly. But they both had the ability to blunt their keen awareness of those words for the sake of self-preservation. It was to be perhaps my most important intervention as a reinstated Guardian Angel and to bring those words forward from memory and to provide a nudge to both Gershom and Artemisia about how those words had enacted damages, post speech. Here is a sampling:

Gershom hears The Pilot:

"Do not cry with your mother. Remember how sick she is."

"Do not cry when you are with her during her last months."

"Stop that. None of that. You are a man now, Ger."

"Get a grip, Ger."

But Gershom cannot utter words and say: "Stop it. Leave me be."

Listen, Gershom, to these words:

By mistakes that were committed before you through having a hard heart.

And for you, Gershom, words fail.

Artemisia hears gossip:

"Do you know what he did on all those business trips?"

"He wanted to do certain things. Do you know what I mean, little one?"

"He sacrificed every, single, thing for you."

"You were always there."

But Artemisia does not say:

"Stop it. Shut up."

Listen, Artemisia, to these words:

For the mistakes committed before you by one who was gathering to do evil.

Words fail for Artemisia.

Gershom says:

"Today, I am a man."

Then Gershom hears:

"Get a grip, Ger."

And Gershom shuts down: Words fail.

Artemisia suffers hearing gossip:

"You were always there."

"What have you done for me lately?"

For the mistakes that were committed before you by degrading your parents.

And Artemisia shuts down. Words fail.

8

Most important for my duties to both of these artists, it would be crucial for me to nudge them into using past memory insights and to draw upon those words, literally, in their art. This is a clear situation of discovering how the inclinations of yetzer-hara may be shifted into inclinations of yetzer-hatov. Turning the harms of words into the beauties of art is what I am getting at here.

The universe is infused with two inclinations. I prefer not to call them "good" and "evil" inclinations but simply two diametrically opposed forces. One force is generally negative, though urgent, and the other force is generally positive, though fragile.

Both of my charges experienced the deaths of their mothers before they were completely evolved into adulthood. The deaths tripped them up, metaphorically. After their happy youths, Gershom flying and floating, Artemisia with gently persistent support from a mother who had the temerity and the insight to put Art right into her daughter's very given name. Both Gershom and Artemisia crash-landed and fell. They did not have the strength to support or to guide or to rationalize the wrenching grief of losing a mother before they were armed with the insights of a few more years.

For all the bar mitzvah claim that: "Today, I am a man," Gershom was only dimly aware of the incandescence of his manhood as it approached. But the shock of loss was so great that, sadly, what got lost was words themselves. And, sadly, the words he received did little to ameliorate his deep psychic wounds. And so, for Gershom, words failed.

The same with Artemisia. The words she heard, then ignored out of self-preservation, were piled upon the recent and very great loss of her mother. She would discover, too soon, how words, *mere,* could destroy. The loss of innocence was, of course, thanks but no thanks, to that gossiping creature, that party-guest who served up rotten nuggets of gossip for Artemisia to ingest. She could not or would not, or maybe elected **not,** to realize, for many years, the damage that was done by words, *mere.* So Artemisia shut down. And for her, words failed.

Chava

1

Yet, in the culture of their lives, as they became adults with jobs and careers and love affairs and making homes, Gershom and Artemisia heard, over and over, the popular notion that *words cannot kill you.*

I am confused. There is just so much that Hannah-Naomi has told me about her charges, Artemisia Gershom and Gershom Holder.

And now, after listening to Hannah-Naomi, I have questions.

2

I wonder: Beyond her being here in my studio — which in itself is questionable — regarding her narratives about being a Guardian Angel, it is not surprising of me to ask further questions:

"Why? How? And then what? And then what?"

I can discern there is more to Hannah-Naomi's story. She shifts. First she thrusts herself off of my sofa, heaving herself up then stretching her arms and wings and legs. Then she wanders around my studio, taking a breather I think. Then she decides on a chair rather than my sofa. She thuds down and rearranges her angelic wardrobe, swings one leg over the other, spins on the wheeled chair to face me, up close, and says to me:

"As students of our Jewish selves it is incumbent that we ask questions. Never just memorize passages. But to engage with questions. So listen to me, Chava. Now I will talk to you about this process in regard to *Al Chet* and to transgressions of the tongue and to how Artemisia and Gershom needed to understand errors of the tongue and to see how transgressions of speech can cause irreparable damage to a person. Both Artemisia and Gershom were told, over and over, in casual admonishment, that they were *too sensitive*. Repeatedly, both Artemisia and Gershom were told: *Words can't hurt you. Words cannot kill.* Yet, remember Chava, that Artemisia heard again and again, throughout her lifetime, the echoes of those wicked words of gossip: "*You were always there. What have you done for me lately?*" And Gershom heard, repeatedly, echoing throughout his lifetime: "*Get a grip, Ger.*" And thus, portions of both Gershom and of Artemisia, were cruelly obliterated."

But now I must ask you, Hannah-Naomi, since you firmly and clearly state that words **can** kill. What do you mean by that? After all, our contemporary human culture asserts that: mere words cannot kill you.

I believe this too: I have said it many times:

"Buck up. Mere words cannot kill you."

Hannah-Naomi

1

That is not true.

Words and words and words — intoned in haste, bitter words, spat out or hissed between clenched teeth — so many brands of hurtful words can cause pain. And, oh yes, they can and do: Kill.

Once a year, at multiple times during the High Holy Days on the Jewish Calendar, members of Synagogues, all over the world, repeat the admonishments of the *Al Chet*. This recitation contains forty-four statements. All members of each congregation stand and repeat aloud and make amends for all forty-four mistakes, or transgressions, or sins — whichever translation you may have. The reading proceeds aloud and, between each point, each and every member of the congregation takes responsibility for making amends and gently taps the heart in repentance:

Tap. Tap.

It does not matter if a single person in the room can say:

"Well, I never did that one. So, I'm clean of that mistake. Whew!"

But that's not how the *Al Chet* recital works. Standing and repeating in unison, and aloud, all forty-four mistakes, means that every single Jewish person takes responsibility for each and every single mistake listed in the *Al Chet*.

The scholars, the rabbis, knew the power of words for destruction and the creation of actual physical harm.

The *Al Chet* is long on specifics addressing the mistakes that can cause harm. It is, however, somewhat of a mystery as to its origins. It may date back to an era during the first diaspora of Secular Jews. Perhaps dating to the destruction of the Second Temple. Perhaps before even that time. When some communities of Jews moved away from the center of the Jewish World, they tried to maintain ritual and observance. And, without the handy instant communication of our present era — if not annoying, those digital modes of information retrieval — citizens in far-away diasporas would write down their questions to the scholars and wise commentators in distant Jerusalem. It must have taken months or years to get responses. The answers to their questions were referred to as *Responsa*. These written responses to the questions are recorded in vast volumes — in numerous books and in documents. *Responsa* have continued throughout Jewish history and may continue right up to the present day in the 21st Century. Some of the *Responsa* were closely held as secret and were communicated by spoken word only. Some were simple enough to be addressed in a single one page letter.

2

Within the *Al Chet*, out of the forty-four statements, fully nine use the word *speech* or imply the way mouths and *speech* are presented as mistakes. Words such as "*endless babbling*" or "*insincere confession*" or "*foolish speech*" or "*vulgar speech*" and "*scornful scoffing*". Taken as a whole, of course, the entire *Al Chet* implies the use of words and language within each of the definitions of all forty-four statements.

Remember this about the *Al Chet*: the congregation, as a whole, stands, and repeats the entire *Al Chet* aloud, together. The congregation, as a whole, takes responsibility, repeating the words of all forty-four *Al Chet* statements with a gentle Tap, Tap, to each and every heart in the congregation as it pays heed to its own responsibility to make next year a better year.

"Yes, Tap, Tap, I take upon my conscience the actions defined very skillfully in the words I am repeating in this moment's recitation of the *Al Chet*. And, even if I, this member of this congregation, have never committed a particular mistake on this very long list, even though innocent, yes, I take heartfelt responsibility for recognizing this form of spoken mistake"

Tap. Tap.

And people still maintain that the spoken word doing

damage, causing pain, and chaos, and you still dare to say out loud and to make your excuse to me that:

"Well it's just words. Words can't kill you."

3

That glib admonishment is not true.

The scholars, rabbis, and wise authors of the *Al Chet* specifically mention the word *speech,* drawing particular attention to the harms that can be done by *mere* speech.

And you still persist in saying:

"Well, mere words cannot kill you."

Well, yes, I must contradict:

In fact: they can. They do.

Kill.

4

I do not mean to harp. I do not speak here by way of sermonizing. But, Chava, you might do well to remember, Angels are prone to harping. We are always in a flap about something.

So listen now to me:

Words, hasty and hot, can kill desire, can kill enthusiasm, can kill inspiration, aspiration, creation. Words, so-called *mere* words, can kill souls and deprive them of the energy needed for a soul's evolution into fulfillment. And a soul is not unlike an Angel — nobody has ever seen one. Yet a soul can be killed. And whether remembered or evoked at a later date by a Guardian Angel who uses memory as a teaching tool, in whatever form and especially spoken loud enough to do their damage, words can kill and have done. I knew this and I saw the power of spoken words to leave indelible damage on the lives of two artists to whom I was tasked with Guardian Angel work. A man and a woman, once children, carrying the wounds of words and words and words. The swift cuts of gossip, so-called, *mere*. Remarks hissed, barely audible, through clenched teeth, snide rejoinders, over and over and over again.

"Get a grip, Ger."

Just words, nevermind. Can't kill you. Right?

5

Words, spoken with a barely audible breath or precisely articulated, shouted even, words will make their mark. Words can hit the unguarded target of a person's heart. And the heart, with its own reasons, may absorb a lifetime's barrage of words as surely as suffering multiple punches to the gut. And those words will pulse and bypass spleen and gall bladder, flying straight into the nearby loyal, ever-beating heart. Eventually such a heart, repeatedly exposed to killing words, the heart, finally, stuttering, can barely function. The heart will however maintain its scars and always has reasons of its own that reason knows nothing of. It may be rational to say:

"Well, it's just words. Words cannot kill you."

But no. The heart retains cruel words, and beats despite pain and injury, beats erratically, barely audible, despite its lifetime burden of words. Words may injure and will endure, for a lifetime — the single lifetime of a single human being — causing injury that may last for decades, leaving the injured human adrift, half dead or, indeed, completely numb, barely conscious, blinded in a dark and numb fugue.

Words have killed. Have killed all kinds of aspiration. Killed dreams. Killed creativity.

I know these things because I have seen and heard the potential for great harm found in words. *Mere* words. Physical harm. Mental harm. Harm to a soul. I have seen words and the harm they may wreck in my charges as I have gone about my duties — for eons — as a Guardian Angel.

6

And one more thing:

Do not mistake words that are spoken in the name of *freedom of speech* as words that are somehow exempt because of some fallacious nobility of motives — do not mistake that kind of freedom with innocence or exemption from harm. Murderous phrases, threats, screamed name-calling, verbal discourtesies, regurgitations of gossip, hollering, words hissed through gritted teeth, yelled in protest, noble protest in the name of *freedom of speech* — all of these and nameless multitudes of other words, *mere*, are capable of creating intense harm, physical and mental. Abused by freedom, so-called, *freedom of speech*:

"I have a right, you know."

Your righteous right, with its ironic twist of good intentions — so-called — is when words can kill most effectively. And they will. And they have done. And they will: kill.

For the mistakes we committed before You through things we blurted out with our lips.

For the mistakes we committed before You through harsh speech.

For the mistakes we committed before You while gathering to discuss negative things.

For the mistakes we committed before You with foolish speech . . . vulgar speech . . . negative speech about others . . . endless babbling . . . telling people what others said about them . . .

For all these, God of pardon, pardon us, forgive us, atone for us our exercise of *freedom of speech*.

Tap. Tap.

7

And for Gershom Holder who heard repeatedly: "Get a grip, Ger":

For the mistake which we have committed before You under duress or willingly; by hard-heartedness; inadvertently; with an utterance of the lips; intentionally or unintentionally; by a haughty demeanor; by a begrudging eye.

Tap. Tap

And for Artemisia Gershom who heard cruel and stinging Gossip:

For the mistake which we have committed before You by running to do evil; by tale-bearing; by hard-heartedness; with an utterance of the lips; with immorality; intentionally or unintentionally; with the evil inclination; knowingly or unknowingly; by evil talk about another; by a haughty demeanor; in passing judgment; by scheming against a fellowman.

Tap. Tap.

Chava

1

Intentionally or unintentionally. Yes, I had not realized that. My doubts. My confusion. I have questioned the very existence of this Guardian Angel in my studio. My words, uttered in doubt and confusion, questioning my own sanity. As usual: I have spoken from the perspective of one living in the Diaspora of the Discombobulated with my glib scoffing and mocking words and words of doubt. All these kinds of words, of speech, I have used in my responses to this Guardian Angel, a visitor in my own rooms.

Hannah-Naomi

1

I have been summoned to the upstairs office. The Creation Director has another assignment for me. Since I am not yet fully reinstated to my Gig Guardian Angel status and able to pick and choose among projects using my own Freewill and while I am on a sort of probation until I can earn back my official designation as a Gig Guardian Angel, I am required to take assignments and to report progress back and forth with the Creation Director as was once my responsibility as a traditional Guardian Angel. Always accountable to this higher authority. Let me see what is next for me from the Creation Director. I sit here at the supernal desk and hear:

"Thus far, Hannah-Naomi, you are doing a credible job getting back into the swing of things with your two charges. I nod to your continuing success in that project. And I recognize that angels can, indeed, multi-task. See how modern I have become? No small credit to your leadership."

I start to kvell, wings a-tremble, at this recognition from the Creation Director.

"Your memory-work with your two Gershoms was, if I may say, a powerful nudge for those two troubled souls. The message that words can be a source of great pain is one that is worthy, alone, of a Yom Kippur sermon."

I need a cigarette.

"Speaking about multi-tasking — well, perhaps we were not — I have an additional project for you, a very pressing need in the universe. I hope you will accept this additional responsibility of certain very special guardianship duties."

I am listening, but I feel a wave of anxiety. Now what? Now what will the Creation Director ask of me?

"The artist, Gershom Holder, who you once fell in love with, and for whom you abdicated your status as an official Guardian Angel to Artemisia Gershom, and with whom you had a brief — I might even say the briefest — of affairs during your rather truncated visit into the body of a human woman — that artist is now in need of guardianship. Many seasons have passed. I want you to see to him, use whatever tools of your trade you can and report back to me when you have completed your job concerning his well-being. Is that clear, Hannah-Naomi?"

"Yes. Abundantly, Creation Director."

It is not without deep misgivings that I take up this project. Not that I have any choice in it. I am still on probation and I urgently desire to be reinstated to my previous Guardian Angel self. Gig worker, with any luck.

But I still do need to prove myself to the Creation Director that I can resume doing a good job as a Guardian Angel and as an independent Gig Guardian Angel. So I take on this project and I answer in the affirmative:

"Yes. I understand. It is clear what needs to be done."

2

I entered this man's studio. There in front of me was this, my one and only, Very Great Love. There he was. Gershom Holder. The Creation Director was right. This man needs me. Needs, rather, a Guardian Angel. This man had been touched by the Angel of Death. This man, my former Very Great Love, was already in extremis. He needed tending now. All I could do was to postpone the impending moment. I had to stifle a rush and then a fever of female human beingness left over in my heart as my foolish, foolish love flared up again to overwhelm my guardianship responsibilities. I knew I loved this man still. Was this a test? Had the Creation Director assigned me to this project to see if I would hold fast to my tentative reinstatement back to true Guardian Angel status? Or would I fall yet again, and losing all of it, succumb, again, to human passions for one of the sons of men? Flying. Falling. Floating.

Would I become a Fallen Angel again?

I could do it. Of course I could. I still had a remaining tool of my trade, hidden in among my other tools, deep inside my Guardian Angel Portfolio. I could put on the mantel of a human being again and resume being a human woman and be with this man for just a few seconds at the end of his life here on this side of The World to Come. I could do it, you know. Yet, too, if I did this thing, I too would die.

Golda

1

We embrace, sprawled and fragile, here together on this old sofa, me now an aging Golden Retriever, treasured companion of my ar-dist, this fading human man. We have lived in this same studio for some goodly number of years. Perhaps more years than would seem possible, whether you count them in dog years or in human ar-dist years. We are old companions, still together, embracing as we are this afternoon in mutual solace for our multitude of aches and pains.

Today we are neither of us feeling well. My hip bones ache and cause me to wobble if I try to wag my tail and walk at the same time. My ar-dist, too, has aching bones, causing him to rock back and forth side-to-side on his two legs when he tries to walk. A couple of wrecks we are. Ah, well.

You ask about the cat?

No?

You did not.

Well, that is okay.

She had a name, too, since you ask: Soixante-Huit. In honor and remembrance of 1968, the year of Les Événements in Paris. That's when my ar-dist took her home to live with us. During Les Événements in France. She was one of the kittens that a friend of his, a French major, needed to find a home for. My ar-dist and I had lots of nicknames for Soixante-Huit — Dees Wheaties, Suzi Soixante, Swee-tweet — tender endearments like that and always recited with a rub behind her ears or, if she rolled over to present her belly, who could resist a soft purr and gentle rumble of that tummy? She purred reflexively every time. Rolled with her belly open so my ar-dist could rub her. She died long ago, but not before leaving us with her final words:

"Je vous remercie de tout coeur. Retablis-toi vite!"

I have no idea what those words mean. She always spoke in her native tongue. We would get the gist of her meanings, but her words were always mysterious, untranslatable, to us.

I nestle as close to my ar-dist as I can and rest my muzzle on his lap. We sit here like this, just breathing.

"You have been such a good companion, Goldie. You are an angel, Goldie. No matter what, after all these years, you were always there."

Oh, if only I could talk, I would talk right now. We have so much yet to say to one another. I feel a surge of his heart blood thumping, pulsing, then more, faintly, in his veins. I hear his blood flowing, even through his denim shirt.

"Well, old girl, my golden girl, what now?"

I am at this moment overcome with a strange shift in the equilibrium of our studio. Something, but what? I sniff the air. The atmosphere, like blurry fog. It is a familiar scent, but from something, or from someone, a remembrance from a long time ago. I tremble. If my hips could function I feel I would need to spin around, first this way, then that way. But as it is, all I can do is tremble and I put my paw on my ar-dist's lap. He seems not to be affected.

2

"Remember, Goldie, that girl I loved? The one who ran away?"

Of course. That is the scent I feel right now. It was that girlfriend who was in heat. And he ran out of the studio. And she stayed and slept 'til morning. Then she fled for a while. She did return for a short visit. Then she left us, left my ar-dist finally and forever. We never saw her again. But love? I did not know my ar-dist loved her. Strange. Then he told me this:

"I could never ta-ta-talk to the girls. I was so af-af-afraid. My throat would just ch-choke up. I would get dizzy. Most girls just ch-ch-chattered, on and on. But I could just not say a single thing. Sometimes I would try. Then I would st-st-st-stutter. Choke again. St-st-st-stutter. And that made things worse for me. I shut down. To speak. Or not to speak. Sometimes they would taunt me and laugh. St-st-st-st st chanting at me. Teasing me. Laughing. Mean, their jokes. St-st-st-st, hissing they would chant. Si-si-si-singsong. Stupid,

me, so stupid. I, I, I . . . and at home, str-str-str-angled. Missing my mom, I, I, I was just a little boy, not a m-m-m-man. . . I, I, I . . . and no, nothing but get, get, get a grip-ip-ip.

"Get-a-grip-Ger."

"And, and, ever since then and all those other t-t-times , m-m-my words fail."

Oh, my ar-dist. I know how that feels. I cannot speak too. I wish I could speak. Right now. I can only make these sounds. Like the first bit of saying something. Then I whimper. Sometimes I can bark, loud and ruff. Ruff. Ruff. Not speaking though. Ru-ru-ruff!

My ar-dist stirs a bit. I feel his heartbeat stutter. He is broken now. Yet for all my skills, I cannot retrieve him now.

"My Golden One. My angel."

Now I feel a warm embrace, but it is not only of my ar-dist's arms around me. It is as if this room, my ar-dist's studio, were engulfed in a strong and warm embrasure, an embracing breeze, and I recognize its sensation as from that very long ago when we were visited by that strange soul, that tangled and perplexed human woman who ran away from my ar-dist. I must tell my ar-dist what I feel. All I can do now, however, is to nudge closer onto his lap. I lick his cheek. He places his hand upon my ribcage. I breathe in and out. I feel my urge to speak but I am wordless. My ar-dist whispers:

"Ah, Goldie,"
And he ruffles my ears:

"My golden, golden angel. You were always here."

3

And now he is gone. I cannot retrieve him now, nor can I forevermore, for all my skills as his beloved Golden Retriever are vanished.

I will not be able to bring him back into our room now, back into this, our studio. I cannot. Trying, I discover: I simply can not.

I must get up now. There is one more thing for me to do. I struggle, at least to stand, then use my legs which drag, hampered painfully by my aching hip bones. My paw pads and my old nails click across our floor, slow, hesitating on this one last walk. I go over to the window and place my nose on the icy windowpane where there are so many nose prints of mine already there, and I rub my nose among the smudges, adding my tears, and I say this:

"Ah, my ar-dist, dear golden friend of mine, I am here and have ever been. For now, good-bye. I have further work to do."

Hannah-Naomi

1

I yearned to have returned to him — my Very Great Love. But I did not. Simply could not. Rather, must not.

I could have put on the mantel of a human woman. If so, I would never return to being a Guardian Angel. If I had done this thing, made myself into a human woman yet again, I would have forfeited eternal life. Then I would have been, again, a Fallen Angel. I would have changed myself for the love of one of the sons of men.

But I did not.

Instead, alone, I will continue toward my reconciliation with being a Guardian Angel and, maybe, I will finally pass these infernal tests that the Creation Director has presented to me. I will, through my own Freewill, complete my tests and return some day, I hope, to being a fully fledged Guardian Angel. Gig worker, of course.

Since you, dear Chava, are still listening to me, I deduce

that you may be somewhat of a believer by now. Yes? And since you obviously listened to the internal dialog of Goldie, the Golden Retriever, even more so does it indicate your acceptance of myth, of your ability to believe in things you cannot see and in voices you cannot hear. So there. I am done.

Yet remember this last:

Angels may take the shape of human beings or of animals.

2

Today, there is an important meeting. The Creation Director has gathered all of us Guardian Angels into the big conference room. There is a huge hand-lettered banner strung from wall to wall:

The Big, Bigger, Biggest Idea Ever

The Creation Director will conduct the meeting and will set forth policies and positioning statements to be used in the near futures of all Guardian Angels. Let us see what this is all about. Here is how our Creation Director starts the exciting, we hope, new announcement:

"I have gathered you here today to tell you about some changes that are taking place these days in the duties and management of the work of Guardian Angels. There has been a radical and unexpected evolution of how your work is to be performed from this day forward. It is called the Gig Economy. This change will affect all human beings: office workers, tillers of the soil, medicine makers, kings, queens, believers and scoffers. But, most importantly, the Gig Economy will radically change how each of you, as Guardian Angels, will work in the future. No longer will human beings work for a single supervisor. So, too, with Guardian Angels. This is what I am here to tell you about, to let you know how today's Gig Economy and its miraculous new tools will affect you as individual professional Guardian Angels. You are about to become Gig Guardian Angels in the vast Gig Economy."

Is this it? Our Creation Director pauses for effect. We Guardian Angels, here in this room today, are deeply tuned in to what our Creation Director is now saying. In fact, we are experiencing just a bit of a sense of déjà vu. It feels like we've already heard all of this some time ago. Only difference is, it is not me, Hannah-Naomi, who is conducting the presentation. My wings are tightly folded across my chest, in silent protest.

Our Creation Director pauses for effect. We Guardian Angels, here in this room today, are deeply tuned in to what our Creation Director is now saying. In fact, we are experiencing just a bit of a sense of déjà vu. It feels like we've already heard all of this some time ago. Only difference is, it is not me, Hannah-Naomi, who is conducting the presentation. My wings are tightly folded across my chest, in silent protest.

Our Creation Director continues with the presentation:

"To keep it simple — instead of your being employed by me, as my heavenly host and your Creation Director, you will henceforth work as free-lancers, in a new business model that is called The Gig Economy. You will all become, as of today, Gig Guardian Angels. In the Gig Economy you will not work for your entire lifetime in a single organization with one single supervisor in charge of your assignments. From now on, you will find yourself using your own Freewill. On your own, you will be tasked with many differing projects, sometimes simultaneously. And you may find yourselves multi-tasking. Guardianship duties will now be called: Gigs. From now on, you will all be gig workers. You will be on your own, make your own decisions, report to no entity except your own heavenly conscience. Understand?"

The Creation Director looks rather pleased with our somewhat muted enthusiasm.

"I knew you would appreciate this 21st Century improvement upon the ways and means of working as Guardian Angels. Over the eons I have noted that Freewill has become the leitmotif of angelic pursuits."

Leitmotif? What? This is crazy talk!

Continuing, our Creation Director puffs up with pride:

"Thus, with only yourselves to report to as you are out working in the field, your duties, and their time and energy, will be streamlined. I knew you would appreciate my idea here and I look forward to hearing from you in the future, not as supreme advisor or boss, but as your — what shall we call it — as your co-equal colleague. I hereby anoint and subsequently give name to this new entity, this new thing on this everlasting earth, "The Creator

Economy." You like? Now I will turn over the meeting to Hannah-Naomi and she will fill you in on some of the new tools of your trade."

And so we are launched into our new lives. Not much has changed, really. We do, perhaps, have rather a long way to go on the topic of giving credit for the creation of our new job description for our duties as Guardian Angels. But later for that. Tomorrow is always another day.

I take to the podium:

"Coffee anyone? Be an angel and get us a cup."

3

And so, Chava, you have patiently listened to my stories, including my opinions about words. Of course these are only opinions. Take no mind if you do not agree with one or any of them.

Here is one last thought: I believe that as a Guardian Angel I was able to nudge my two Gershoms back into life. As Gershoms, both, they experienced many coincidences. Almost twins, they had coincidences of their names. They had coincidences of untimely grief. Coincidentally, they suffered words that kill. I nudged them into memory work until they could finally **get** the necessity of life-saving and soul-enhancing work. Their work demanded that they leave behind their father's words. Leaving things behind are prophetically summed up and universally applicable, as seen in L'ech Lecha: ". . . *leave your father's house for the land I will show you.*"

Chava

1

And, just like that, she is gone.

Without good-bye, no peck on the cheek, Hannah-Naomi is gone. She is suddenly no more. Not on my sofa. Not in my studio. Nowhere. Gone.

I cannot express how lonesome this feels.

I feel so still. So silent. The silence of nothingness.

Not even my own fears, for my own sanity, do I feel. Yet I must be nuts. Is that right? What kind of mild impairment of my brain's cognition created this very definite visitor, this Hannah-Naomi, Gig Guardian Angel? What just happened?

I can't believe it.

Can I?

Or, can I, yes, believe this apparition appeared then disappeared.

Do I believe it?

Or not?

ARTEMISIA'S STUDIO FIFTY YEARS LATER

IT ALL STARTED when I was in my late sixties. Around that time, I started to do what turned out to be, a memory review. Suddenly some of my old memories began to take on new meanings. It was as if I finally **got** what past events actually meant. This memory review was not always pleasant. Far from it. But my new interpretations of my own ancient history, shook me, startled me, then shoved me in a new direction in my studio.

Funnily enough, I also recalled trivial past events — old crushes I had had in the university art department, senior year. Like that guy called Gershom. Weird coincidence, our names. Strong silent type. Ridiculous. I hadn't thought about him for fifty years.

Anyway, during my memory purge, for some unknown reason I started a series of paintings featuring a character I call Goose Girl. Don't know exactly why. So familiar they feel. I love them. I love viewers cannot guess what they contain.

My paintings are are all flying, falling, floating. Where to? I wonder. Paintings may foretell the future or the past. They may take the shape of human beings or of animals. May be formed of half fire and half water. A painting may have no evil intentions — it is simply what may be seen. God knows paintings are not perfect. That's not the point. Most times paintings cannot, will not, answer questions.

These, in particular: I have made many Goose Girl paintings. Are they mine? Or about me? Or simply: are they only *allowed* to me? Or is that Goose Girl me? Or someone else?

Paintings may, or may not have, both angelic and demonic forces. Human beings may surround themselves with paintings that they may interpret as having energy for both protection and for healing. But a painting may or may not help, protect, nor heal its viewer. Same goes for its creator, me the artist. The only impediments to connecting with a painting's energy are doubt and cynicism. Or literalism. Or viewing the works with intentional intellectual eyes in the belief that rationalizing or explaining or questioning the art will reveal its content, its meaning. A viewer may ask: what does this painting mean? The title may or may not reveal meaning. But why ask? The painting may or may not reveal literal truth. Literal meaning. Literal interpretation. Who cares? Just look. Look. What do you see? Look.

So many sure things are written about paintings. Technique. Historical references as to genre. Who is currently painting like Franz Kline? Or Van Gogh? Who wants Picasso out because he beat his women? The artist's destiny? I leave that to the scholars. No matter what they think, pro or con — they surely will have a lot to say either way — who gives a fig? Is a puzzlement. Yes?

— Artemisia Gershom

GERSHOM'S STUDIO
TEN YEARS AFTER COLLEGE GRADUATION

I COULD ALWAYS WRITE. I had no trouble with my words with typewriter, pencil, computer — given any tool of the trade for writing and I am fine. Given a ream or two of blank paper, I will go on and on, garrulous.

But talk?

My throat seizes up. I feel it. I get a grip in my throat. I try to cough it out. No relief. Then my heart skips and stutters several beats, one on top of another. Of course, as I got older, I learned that this symptom was named heart arrythmia. How clever was that bit of naming — I mean the double rr — so much in imitation of what was actually happening in a heart. And the heart seizes up and rr, rr, rr, rr — one heartbeat right on top of the last heart beat — a rat-a-tat-tat inside the chest of the arrythmiaator. A brilliant use of onomatopoeia in the spelling of a word, yes? And so, dutifully, I volunteer for a ration of heart tests and not one proved to be anything clinical that could be diagnosed for my stuttering heartbeat.

But, as you can see, I can always write.

As an artist I could also draw on what I have learned, draw from what life has given me. My paintings: may take the shape of animals. A painting takes no action without a command to look and look.

A few years ago, out of nowhere in particular, I began to paint animals: dogs mostly.

To be fair, the only way I wanted to serve them — dogs, I mean — is to put out their bowls of food, day after day, and to toss a grimy chartreuse tennis ball across my studio and to watch, not with bowing down, but with loving fondness. You see? And my dog trots back to me, slobbering all over that tennis ball which she holds securely between her top teeth and her lower canines. I weasel the ball out of her drooling grip and roll her over as we laugh and I tickle her ribcage. She has a firm grip on my love and her golden eyes laugh with me, my Golda, my beautiful golden girl is always there when I need her. She is an angel.

When I finally graduated from school I found a huge sunny open room in a crumbling industrial building — cheap, not very clean, but mine. Now I was an art major with a degree and I needed to get a grip on everything in my whole life, me, with my tongue, stuck, but my heart still beating.

Well, so of course, I worked to get a fine clean grip on my studio space and I spent a few weeks cleaning floors, washing the myriad windowpanes, which brought sunshine in from the east and from the south. And I even purchased a wise stock of toilet paper — toilet paper being the most prized possession of an artist for his female guests and sadly missing from many studios where men paint, round the clock, Serious Painters, with minds upon higher things than human excretions and female comfort. Oh yes, the men who I knew who painted had much more important things to consider than the paucity of toilet paper in their studios. I knew this. Women who visited my studio told me how they loved my ample shelves with those little white rolls, clean rolls I might add, all lined up, wrapped in tissue paper in my studio bathroom. I and my toilet paper were favored far and wide with the women.

I paint animals. Well, animal forms. Not portraits. Not hair by hair of fur against bone structure as you see. I paint birds with broken wings. Take these broken wings and learn to fly. I know about broken wings. I know about that kind of flight that flaps, frantic and repetitive, the kind of broken flight that could send the bird spinning downwards towards the ground, unable to get a grip with flying, landing instead on the ground, crashing, silenced, silent.

Blackbird broken at the break of day, take these broken wings and learn to fly and look and look at heaven above, and earth beneath, and at water under the earth. Such beauty. Beauty. Words fail.

— *Gershom Holder*

Author's Commentary

1

What is the harm of a human being believing in Guardian Angels? Likewise, what is the harm if a human being does *not* believe in Guardian Angels? I ask you.

You might also ask this of Hannah-Naomi. She'll have a thing or two to say about both of those beliefs:

"Sure, I guess I would worry if someone built an alter in her kitchen, replete with little candles, sticks of incense, twigs of lavender, offerings to that kitchen Guardian Angel. And, if subsequently, this woman, cooking in her own kitchen, recited incantations while stirring the gravy, well then, maybe I would quibble. If I were the Creation Director, I can see that that kind of worship could cause some concern — bowing down to false gods and all of that. Or how about this: plain old jealousy on behalf of the one and only Creation Director? Remember the singularity of this Creation Director — this god is a jealous

god. But I harp."

Harp! You like it!?

So I say this: what harm is done with belief in Guardian Angels? Same with dis-belief: what harm is done?

But where have all the angels gone now?

Look at this date. There are none. Not now.

And the scoffers, winners now in this debate, they spit at me:

"See! See! There are no such entities."

How sad.

Where have all the angels gone?

So then, why, exactly, did the mothers and grandmothers whisper to the children:

"You have a Guardian Angel"

They did not say this to the children to indoctrinate them to one or another form of religious observance. They said this to their children to imbue them with a sense of protection, of security. They whispered gently into those little ears and the children's eyes grew wider and wider at the wonder of their secret:

"I have a Guardian Angel."

It was to protect, to help sustain physical and mental comfort, even to stave off scary nightmares that awaken children in the night. That is why the mothers and grandmothers whispered:

"You have a Guardian Angel."

Well, the world has changed hasn't it?

—

2

Before I started this project, I asked a variety of my friends if they believed in Guardian Angels or not. The responses were a surprise. Half did. Half did not.

So where did the mythos of the Guardian Angel come from? It resides across cultures and throughout every religion from Anglicanism to Zoroastrianism. And whether the various scholars of these religions are believers or not believers, they are united in the fierceness of their arguments, pro or con. They write voluminously, fine and well-constructed rhetoric, coming from either side of this mysterious topic. They take very seriously their belief or non-belief. So what's the big deal? I mean, it's not like talking about peace or justice or ethics or morals — it does not have the heft of those evermore serious human concerns. Big stuff, you know. Talking about Guardian Angels may be talking about an unseen, unproven, immaterial entity that is not really an entity at all. Pixies, gnomes, elves, goblins, sprites, fairies, little folk. Angels, archangels, fallen angels. Flying, falling, floating — are they for real or are they mere figments? Or are they, perhaps, safer to talk about than that other unseen entity: God?

Oh, for heavens' sake!

Here's a thought: maybe this is what it is all about: Loneliness.

Maybe it is a myth inborn of the human psyche. Developed in lonesomeness, inside the mind of the miniscule earthbound creatures that we are, residing in frangible human bodies, standing under the all-too-spangled starry, starry night, looking upward into unfathomable dark matter. So, naturally, the measly, fragile human creature needs — has perhaps, an insufferably deep and shuddering need — for a sidekick, someone, or something, always on your side, as protector, partner, trusted advisor, invisible sprite, a shield, there to serve and protect. A dog? Perhaps. A god? Well, nevermind gods; that's way too complicated, fraught with doctrine and hell and all such. Dangerous too, that topic.

How sad. How desolate to feel oneself lone among some. Lone-some. How then, to solve this lonesome plight? And thus the idea of Guardian Angels strikes such a resonant chord, addresses such an urgent need, in the minds of scholars and of my random list of friends and in their hearts. The believers find solace, are comforted. The non-believers are testy, annoyed by such foolishness, can function just as well without a Guardian Angel, thank you very much. All of these opinions. All of these perspectives. All over the single topic of Guardian Angels that nobody, nobody, has seen or not seen. Ever.

3

I have in storage a battered old box of my parents' war letters. There is also a very worn out, old manila folder with another small group of later letters. In it were some of my own college letters, somehow saved by my mother. There were also copies, plus the originals, of some letters that my mother wrote to her mother in August and September of 1968 — just days before she died. How these letters were copied and by whom and how the originals were also included in the folder, I do not know. The serendipity eludes me, but if I were to believe in a Guardian Angel, I might credit the coincidence of reading these letters, along with my mother's war letters with — with what? With tending to believe in my own personal Guardian Angel, nudging me?

Remember: *You have a Guardian Angel.*

And in this tattered folder was this letter written in my own mother's school teacher's handwriting:

20 August 1968

They are so wonderful in caring for me.Day after day when I had to go to my treatment one of them would drive me there . . . they spoil me terribly . . .

They take such good care of me . . . they are like angels.

And, Hannah-Naomi interrupts me, right now, with:

"There! There! You see?Proof positive that:Angels may take the shape of human beings".

You are a very clever Guardian Angel, Hannah-Naomi. Creative in your own defense. Now you want to claim the last word on belief in YOU.

I am still ambiguous.

Yes, seeing my mother's letter was a shock to me and it came to my attention so many years later. I got that box of war letters — plus that battered folder of miscellaneous letters from my mother — I received those letters when I was fifty. Was it a coincidence? A message from the beyond? I cried. Yes, I did cry when I saw her words. But discovery of her words in that letter, was coincidence, mere coincidence. Granted, it felt like a message directly from her to me.

4

I will need to think about that some more. Was that letter shoved to me by my own Guardian Angel? Was it a nudge from her? And why so many years later? I wish I had known about that letter when I had been much younger. Does my discovery of those words imply that it was I who became a Guardian Angel?

Well. I still do not know how I come out on the belief, or disbelief, in Guardian Angels. And I am baffled by the appearance in my life of Hannah-Naomi. In my studio. In *real* life. Talking on and on. She was a talker, that's for sure. Telling me all about her life as a Guardian Angel. Filling me with the facts and experiences of her supernal existence. Still. Still, I have to ask: was she just an hallucination? Am I slipping into brain-damaged visions? Did she or did she not visit me in my studio? Talk to me? Slouch into my sofa? Did Hannah-Naomi really exist? I wonder.

I cross the room into the bathroom. I stand in front of the big full length mirror. For more than seven decades of wear and tear, I still look pretty okay. I shower, wash my hair. I get dressed. I am relatively tidy for an old, maybe senile, old lady. Who am I? What just happened to me? Where did Hannah-Naomi come from? Who was she? WAS she? I conclude with this: It very much does not matter whether people believe or do not believe in Guardian Angels does it? But, for whatever reasons, it is predictable that there will be two very opinionated opinions:

Yes,

Or

No.

Right?

Now I tend to think: Yes. But I cannot tell you why. I feel discombobulated.

The lilting and cranky particularity of French sums up this conundrum with:

"Le cœur a ses raisons que la raison ne connat point." *"The heart has its reasons, for which reason knows nothing of."*

— END—

"A book grows according to a subtle and deep-laid plan. At the end, I see what the plan was."

— Hilary Mantel

Author Afterword

Thank you first readers, particularly this time around. Being a first reader for a friend can be fraught with peril. You do not want to lose a friendship if you cite definite problems with a manuscript. You do not want to lose a friendship if you neglect to cite problems. If you are simply being kind and generous in your commentary, the ungrateful author might bristle at mere flattery. You just can't win as a first reader. There are simply too many perils in the life of a first reader. Well, just this for each of you — I love you, still, and I love you even more when you were bold and true in your observations – I needed that. And, most of all, each of you is blessed with significant levels of patience:

"What? Another go-round? Another iteration of your last manuscript for me to read? Sure. Love to!"

What made this novel so hard to write? Why so many iterations of this manuscript?

I offer this apologia because this book was particularly difficult for me. In order to make this fiction true, I needed to do a great deal of background research: reading about angels, pro and con; discovering what many religions believe about angels; learning attitudes toward angels down through history; turning to books and books and books and websites galore; and then deriving meaning from that work. At times I was so boggled, so overloaded, I could not think straight. Why the heck did I want to write about angels in the first place? And most importantly, how could I possibly make fiction out of something that so many people already believe is FICTIONAL? 'twas a puzzlement.

There were other problems which required a re-thinking of the manuscript as well. The working title: I discovered that there were literally dozens of books with the same title. So I changed the title. That required restructuring my narrative and relevant themes. THEN: when I googled the female name for my angel, the first entry I discovered turned out to be a link to a porn website. Sheesh! Oh for heaven's sake! Off I went revising yet again. And, of course, the new name for my angel character required many picky little edits and some substantive story changes. Now I was calling the manuscript a *thing* — for now I was not certain it would ever be a book. It was enough for me to start to believe in a guardian angel doing everything she could do to keep me from writing this book!

I'm not complaining. But it hasn't been easy.

Thank you to everyone who helped point me in the right direction about angels: Bob, Sharon, Mark, Perri, Natalie, Diane, Norma, Alisha, Deborah, Laura, Allison, Joann, Teresa and Jim and many others who took the time to answer "yes" or "no" to my persistent question: Do you believe in guardian angels? And thanks to my editor, Allison Smith – patient with me throughout much discombobulation. And of course to my husband, Gary W. Priester, bearing up with me as both wife and client for designing my books.

With love in these times,
— Mary

Selected References

An Inquiry Into the Existence of Guardian Angels, Pierre Jovanovic

The Guide of the Perplexed, Moses Maimonides

Encyclopaedia Judaica, Volume 2: Angels and Angelology

The Zohar, Pritzker Edition, Daniel C. Matt

The Soul, Rabbi Adin Even-Israel Steinsaltz

God Is a Verb, Kabbalah and the Practice of Mystical Judaism, Rabbi David Cooper

Babylonian Talmud, Tractate Sanhedrin

The Hebrew Bible, Translation With Commentary, Robert Alter

The Torah A Women's Commentary, URJ Press

Accepting Voices, Marius Romme and Sandra Escher

The River of Consciousness, Oliver Sacks

Artemisia, Latizia Treves

www.aish.com

www.chabad.org

www.jewishvirtuallibrary.org

www.wikipedia.org

History of Responsa in Judaism

The Creator Economy

www.myjewishlearning.com

www.reformJudaism.org

www.oxfordreference.com

www.torah.org

www.beliefnet.com/faiths/judaism

www.ou.org/torah

tailendcharlietedchurch.wordpress.com/raf-stations/77-squadron — US Flying Schools/Ted Church

Introduction to Mary E. Carter's novel *Diaspora of the Discombobulated*

When we meet Chava she is puzzling over the responses she has received from her friends to her question: Do you believe in Guardian Angels? She observes that half said "yes" and half said "no". What is interesting to Chava is that both types of respondents had many rationales for their responses. Why? For example: she wonders, why would someone who does not believe in Guardian Angels have so many reasons for that position? These responses to her question leave her somewhat baffled.

Then, all of a sudden, she is joined in her studio by a genuine Guardian Angel. This Guardian Angel sets out to tell Chava all about her life as a Guardian Angel. She has quite a story to reveal. Plus, this Guardian Angel has plans to modernize the work of all Guardian Angels, to streamline their functions to better suit the current Gig Economy.

In the continuing back-and-forth of chapters, Chava and the her visitor, Guardian Angel Hannah-Naomi, take turns talking. Chava asks questions. And Hannah-Naomi — in her own roundabout way, answers. Sometimes it is very confusing to Chava, not least because she is afraid she might be losing her mind. After all — who has ever seen or talked to a real Guardian Angel in real life?

Questions for Discussion

Do you believe in Guardian Angels?
If so, why?
If not, why not?

Do you have friends who disagree with your opinion? If you do, how do you approach the subject? Do you discuss further or do you avoid further discussion?

If you believe in Guardian Angels, can you relate an instance when you were assisted or protected by one?

If you do not believe in Guardian Angels, what do you think about the person's reasons who answered the above question?

Do you feel that words can do the kind of serious damage that the Guardian Angel Hannah-Naomi believes they can do?

What do you think or feel during the annual recitation of the *Al Chet*?

Have you ever been seriously hurt by so-called *mere* words?

Have you ever been hurt or damaged by gossip?

If so, can you share your feelings here in this reading group?

Did any of you have parents who were in the military during war – WWII, Vietnam, etc.? If so, did you have any experience with the returning soldiers being distant or abstracted parents?

Do you engage with Torah during study groups — asking questions or making observations of your own? Or do you prefer to listen and think about what others may be saying?

Other than observance of High Holy Day services, do you have any other personal study of Jewish scholarship during the rest of the year?

About the Author

Mary E. Carter was born in the San Fernando Valley before there were freeways. It was a time of dirt roads and orange groves. She had a long career as an advertising copywriter doing TV, radio, and print advertising for everything from dog food to banks to high technology. Carter's award-winning novels include: FINALIST for Debut Novel from National Jewish Book Awards for her novel *I, Sarah Steinway* and WINNER in the New Mexico-Arizona Book Awards for her novels: *All Good Tova Goodman Revised Edition* and *The Three-Day Departure of Mrs. Annette Zinn.* Mary E. Carter lives and works in Placitas, New Mexico.

www.mary-carter.com

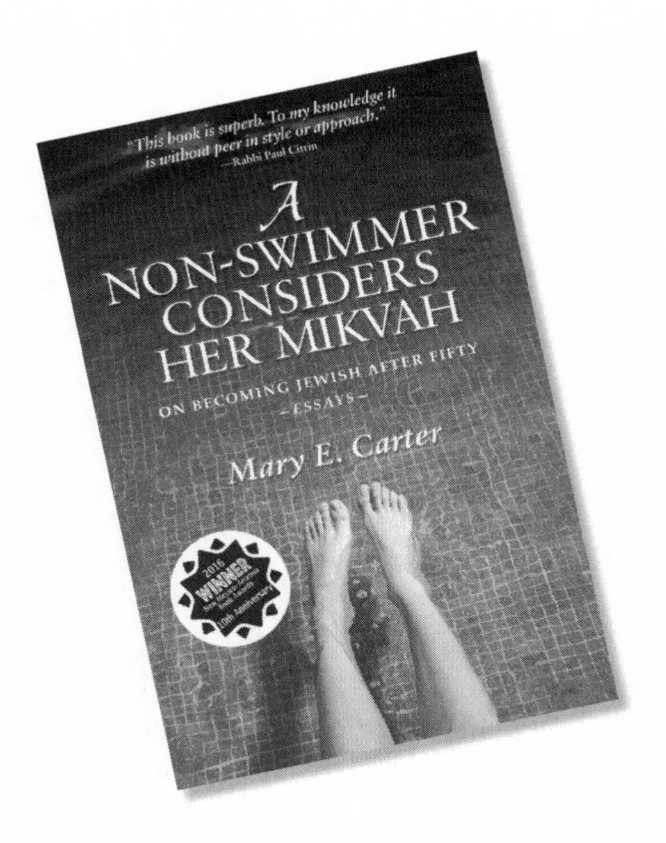
"This book is superb. To my knowledge it is without peer in style or approach."
—Rabbi Paul Citrin
A NON-SWIMMER CONSIDERS HER MIKVAH
ON BECOMING JEWISH AFTER FIFTY
—ESSAYS—
Mary E. Carter
2016
WINNER

Sarah Steinway, aged seventy-five, survives a catastrophic flood by moving into her treehouse on the northern shoreline of the San Francisco Bay. With snark and pluck, she lives up there for five years. Turning to Torah for comfort, she instead engages in argumentation with God, shouting the eternal question: "Why me?"

". . . by turns very funny and very serious,
confident and uncompromisingly weird. Mary E. Carter
has a voice with unquestionable power, and we look
forward to reading more from her."

—Jewish Book Council

Available through Ingram and amazon.

Whatever happened to Sarah Steinway? Find out in this sequel, *All Good Tova Goodman Revised Edition*. Readers will be surprised by the haunting conclusion of Mary E. Carter's Award-Winning Debut Novel, *I, Sarah Steinway*.

> *"Carter's page-turning portrait of a woman surviving the apocalypse is hauntingly memorable."*
>
> — Publishers Weekly

Available through Ingram and amazon

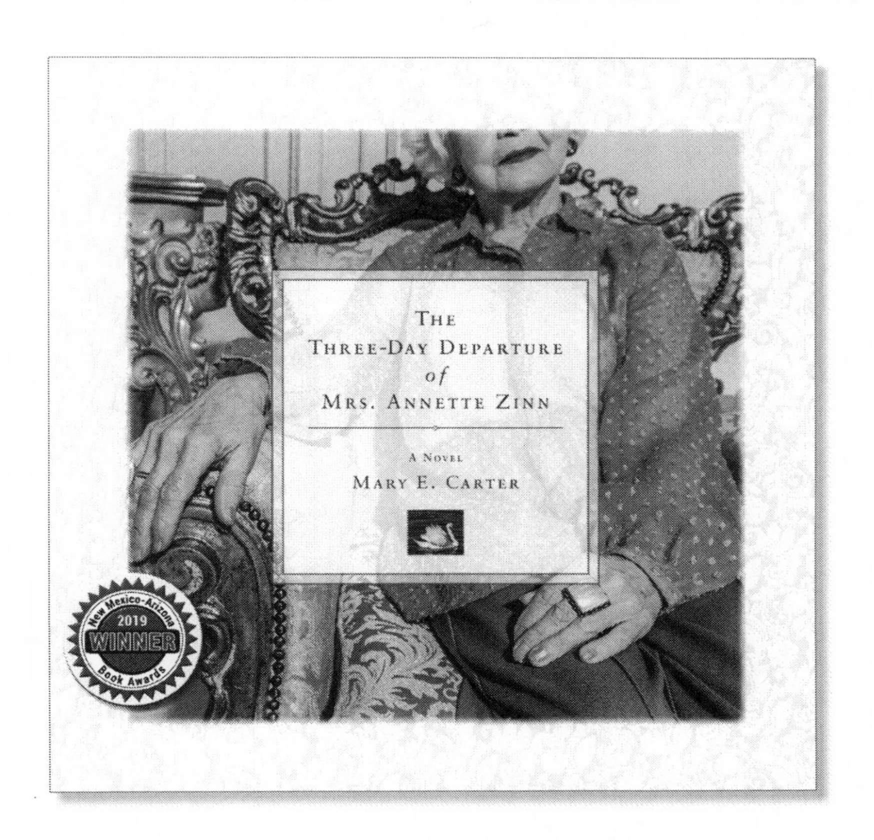

"I always look forward to getting to know Mary E. Carter's characters. The Jews, and the righteous non-Jews as well, have a pintele yid: a spark of Jewishness that helps them navigate this complex world with sensitivity. I enjoyed the exploration of the soul hovering for three days and was intrigued with the idea that it might remember details of events that were forgotten or hidden during its time in this world. During her three-day departure, Mrs. Annette Zinn discovers that her memories have the potential to serve as a blessing."

— Rabbi Jack Shlachter
Judaism for Your Nuclear Family, phisicsrabbi@gmail.com

Available through Ingram and amazon

Made in the USA
Middletown, DE
17 July 2023